M000190093

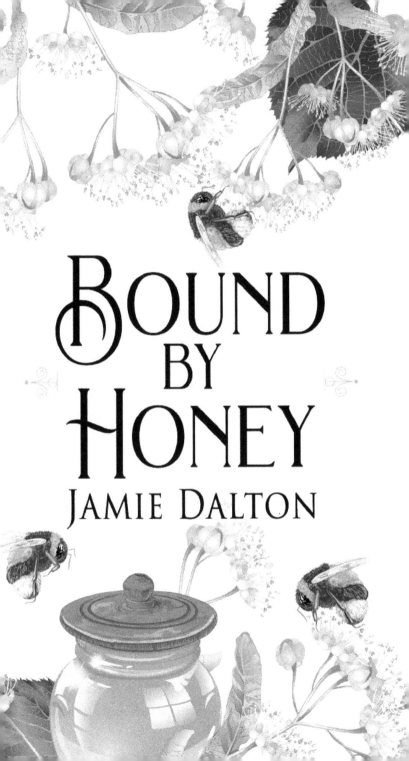

BOUND BY HONEY

JAMIE DALTON

Cover Designed by Cover Dungeon Rabbit

Art Under Hardcover Dust Jacket by Christina Schneider

***To see all books written by Jamie Dalton or her spicy alter ego J. D. Magnetra or

for any reqsts go to www.jamiedalton.net

Contents

Twinkle, Twinkle, Little Dragon

S age sipped on her white chocolate lavender latte, listening to the screams of her fellow li-
brarians and patrons. She could see books flying
above the distant shelves on the second floor from
her seat in the coffee shop near the entrance. A
man in the royal palace's green robes darted from
the shelves toward the balcony railing, only to be
smacked on the back of the head with a rather thick
leather-bound book, resulting in a loud *thunk*. The
man face-planted onto the polished wood floor.

"Are you going to help them?" her best friend,
Piper, asked.

She smiled and took another sip. "Not until I finish
this. Let them learn not to mess with the restricted
section before I save them ... again."

Piper glanced up at the balcony, tucked an escaped
chestnut brown curl back into place, and chuckled
as she began wiping the tables.

It had only been two months since Sage started at
the Royal Library for the Public Citizens of Sarash,
and from her first cup of coffee served to her by
Piper, she knew they would become close friends.

Sage downed the rest of her drink much faster than she would have liked and carefully set the delicate, blue-and-white cup on the table. It was her favorite among the coffee cups used. Her heart sank at the thought of something happening to it. With a heavy sigh, she rose from her chair and walked toward the stairs.

The Royal Library for the Public Citizens of Sarash was magnificent in its design, from the grand arched doorway to the window-covered walls, each with a full complement of shelves.

The polished dark wood stairs glowed under the twin crystal chandeliers that hung on fine silver chains. Sage took the stairs two at a time on her way to the restricted section. Her breath came harder as she smelled the musk of old books, the aroma of old leather and ink. The smell of knowledge, wisdom, and power.

Sage ducked under a rogue-flying book before heading toward the section's center. This happened anytime someone tried removing a book from the restricted section. She was slightly out of breath when she got there.

It was really a very simple process to let Freddie the gargoyle, who ran this section, scan the book and your identification. He slept during the day anyway, and while his appearance was quite intimidating, he couldn't move. The sign next to him was clear.

To check out books from the restricted section, please place one book at a time in my right hand and your identification on my left. Sing Twinkle, Twinkle, Little Dragon once before removing both. Repeat the process for up to three books. All books are due back in one week. If you have forgotten the words to Twinkle, Twinkle, Little Dragon, they are as follows:

> *Twinkle, twinkle, little dragon*
> *If you're hungry, eat a sheep*
> *Up above the world so high*
> *Soaring, flying in the sky*
> *Twinkle, twinkle, little dragon*
> *If you're hungry, eat a sheep*

For each book after the first, please change the animal you feed your dragon. Remember to always start with a sheep, though. They are most dragons' favorite food.

Your Friendly Gargoyle Librarian,
Freddy

By the time Sage approached Freddy, most of the individuals had escaped. The books floated high above the empty shelves, waiting for their next target. Freddy knew she was there based on the fact they no longer aimed at her.

While technically frozen in stone during the day, his magic still ran this section smoothly. At night all books were put back in their place, and her antisocial friend could read to his heart's content without a soul in sight. A sentiment she understood completely.

Approaching Freddy, she placed her hand on his shoulder, and an image appeared before him as books began falling around her. A fae man with long, black hair and a grey tunic embroidered in silver carried *The Book of Carnivorous Plants and Other Hungry Things* under his arm. If she wasn't mistaken, he was heading toward the exit next to the coffee shop.

"I will be back in a moment to start cleaning this up, Freddy! Sorry about the mess!" she yelled as she hurried to catch the book thief.

Her dark brown hair and white skirts billowed behind her as she ran to the stairs, then slid down the railing. As soon as her feet hit the floor, she took off running, only to be stopped by a crowd of women blocking her way.

A quick jump up, and the top of the head she was looking for was visible above the crowd.

Sage elbowed her way into the group. "Stop! Let me through!"

Two women pushed her back behind them.

"We were here first!" one of them snapped.

"Working here doesn't give you an excuse to cut in front of us to see the Charming Four," the other added.

Sage had no idea who the Charming Four was, but she would not let anyone disappear with one of her books. Dropping to her knees, she crawled through the crowd until an opening appeared.

Standing up, she came face to face with a solid chest of familiar grey.

"Can I help you?"

Her eyes rose to find muscular shoulders, a square jaw, and the most arrogant smirk she had ever seen on any man. Three other men stepped up behind him. The four towered over her, making her heart drop to her stomach.

Her bravery had abandoned her. What had she done?

Sage's eyes flitted down to the hands of the man in front. They held no book.

She panicked and pushed him to the side.

Her eyes scrutinized the man on the left. His straight red hair was half pulled back, revealing high cheekbones and bright blue eyes wide in surprise.

His hands were empty, though.

She could feel the muscles in her neck tighten as she became more stressed.

Standing in the middle was the tallest of the four. His dark brown eyes held only sympathy as he took in her panic.

She was disappointed to find that his hands were also empty. Sage wanted to cry.

The man on the end appeared to find this entire situation funny. Sure, she might seem a bit excessive to some, but she would lose her dream job if she lost one of these books.

Sage desperately wanted to wipe that smug smirk off his beautiful tanned face. His short blond hair, violet eyes, and petal-pink lips made him look so perfect he almost didn't look real.

A glance down at his hand revealed the familiar, brown, leather book.

She pointed at it. "You can't leave with that book!" she yelled.

Without hesitation, the blond man raised an eyebrow. "I will return it later."

Sage glared at him, her jaw set in determination.

"No, you have to either go back upstairs and check it out with Freddy or give it back now," she insisted.

The handsome stranger only shook his head and laughed.

"I'm afraid I can't do that," he replied calmly.

Angered and frustrated, she lunged at him and tried to snatch the precious book.

He easily sidestepped her, but her fingers connected with the book's bottom. She latched on, refusing to let go.

"Give it back!" she yelled in a panic.

"I'm sorry, but I can't," he replied again without a care in the world.

"Can't or won't?" she spat.

A dimple appeared on his right cheek as he chuckled. "Perhaps a bit of both?"

The book disappeared into thin air with a flick of his long fingers.

Sage gaped at him as she tried to think of some way to get him to give her back the book.

"You can't take the book! It is property of the royal family!" she threatened.

The man once again shook his head and laughed.

"That's cute," he said sarcastically, looking down at her with a smirk.

"I won't let you leave with the book. I have to have it back." Her hands went to her hips.

To her surprise, he shrugged, turned on his heels, and left the library. The three other men followed him. As they walked away, Sage was very aware of the crowd's eyes still surrounding her. Their glares and whispers only made her failure sting even worse.

"Sage?"

Will's voice broke through her thoughts, and she spun to face him.

"What just happened?" he asked, looking just as confused as she felt.

Shaking her head, Sage tried to make sense of it all. "I don't know. They just came in and took the book."

"Did you try to stop them?"

"Of course I did!" she snapped, feeling defensive.

Will held up his hands in surrender.

Sage sighed and ran a hand through her hair. "I tried to stop them, but they were too fast. They just took the book and left."

"Did they say anything?"

"The blond fae said he would return it later," she replied bitterly.

Her friend frowned. "Who do they think they are?!"

"They're the Charming Four." Piper's voice made Sage jump. "The top mage guild in the kingdom. Every guy wants to be like them, and every girl wants to be with them."

"That doesn't give them a right to show up here and act like they own the place," Will replied.

"Technically, it does."

From the look on Piper's face, Sage could tell she wouldn't like this.

"The blond carrying the book is Colby. The oldest son of the Duke of Tishire. The redhead is his cousin, Sawyer. He's the third in line to inherit Brinedin. Both are ice mages who are quite literally as cool as their magic. Asher is the one whose eyes are like melted chocolate you want to sink right into. He has no title but is from a family far richer than the other two as the heir to a collection of gem mines. His earth magic is legendary."

The reality of what she had just done was starting to sink in.

"And the grumpy one?" she whispered.

Piper's grin spread from ear to ear, and her eyes gained a far-off look, "He's the king's third son, Finn. A fire mage. His magic is far more powerful than his older brothers. I heard he wiped out an entire invading army on his own. Just roasted them up like marshmallows."

Will pretended to retch. "Ewww... Thanks for the visual. Thanks to you, I don't know if I can eat marshmallows again."

"You're welcome!" Piper replied with a wink. "I can't believe we got to see them."

"Why's that?"

"Usually, they are out on secret missions for the king, and when they're home, they stick to themselves other than when they're dating only the most beautiful girls in the city."

Sage couldn't help rolling her eyes. "Great, so now I look ridiculous."

Piper shrugged. "You're cute when you're ridiculous," she added with a smile that Sage returned weakly. "You'll get over it. Just learn from your mistakes and don't do it again. They're not worth risking your reputation."

"Easy for you to say," Sage muttered.

She eyed the empty shelves and piles of books on the second floor that still needed to be cleaned up. With a goodbye wave, Sage made her way to the restricted section. Hopefully, her superiors would only write her up if they even heard about it.

With any luck, she wouldn't see the Charming Four ever again, and this would all become a distant memory.

***

Sage loved the smell of her mother's office. It smelled like the library but better.

Vanilla-and-clove-scented candles sat on the large oak desk. A copper dragon split in half at the corner of the desk created the illusion of flying through the real prize in the room. Her mother's books she had written and published herself.

Growing up, Sage had always been so proud of her. It took her years to understand why telling anyone that her mother was an author was forbidden. The local baker's look would forever be burned in her memory after telling him at the innocent age of five that her dear sweet mother, Emma, was, in fact, romance author Lily Lovemate. Afterward, they only ate bread they made themselves to avoid returning until the old man died four years later and his daughter took over the shop.

Tiptoeing across the squeaky floorboards, Sage wrapped her arms around the shoulders of the woman sitting at the desk and offered a quick peck on the cheek.

A warm ink-stained hand grasped hers with a gentle squeeze. "You're home late."

The chair spun, and Sage stared at a slightly older version of herself. While she may have gotten her father's mind for potions, there was no doubt which of her parents Sage looked the most like.

Sage straightened and scratched the back of her head while avoiding eye contact. "I had an incident at work that needed to be taken care of before I could come home."

As much as her mother's knowing look drove her crazy, Sage was thankful her parents weren't the type to pry. They knew if Sage wanted them to know, she would tell them, and in the twenty years of her life, she had worked hard to keep that trust.

"Have you eaten yet?" her mother asked.

Almost as if on cue, Sage's stomach growled, and the two of them laughed.

Placing a quill on the desk behind her, she rose and put an arm around Sage's shoulder. "Let's go find your father and eat. I have broccoli cheddar soup ready for us."

They made their way to the kitchen, where Sage eagerly inhaled the smell of fresh bread waiting to be warmed up.

As her mother opened the bread box, Sage moved to the stove to dish up a bowl of the creamy soup. Her father entered and filled three cider mugs before sitting at the table.

"Sage, honey, come here. We need to talk about something."

Sage walked over and sat in a chair at their dining table. She knew whatever this was about, she wasn't going to like it. Her father never called her by her first name.

A plate of bread dropped onto the table with a loud thunk. A mumbled sorry escaped her mother's lips as she slid into the seat beside Sage.

"What's wrong?" Sage asked. Her parents were usually calm and collected. The fact that they were anxious only made her own worse.

"Your father and I have been talking, and we need to know if you plan on moving out on your own."

Sage was shocked.

"I didn't realize there was a time frame I needed to move out in."

Her mother placed her hand over Sage's. "Oh, no, dear, that's not what this is about."

Both women gave her father an expectant look.

He cleared his throat. "I have been offered an opportunity ... for work. But it would require us to move. We would still be on the main island, but several days' journey away. Your mother can work from anywhere, and we thought since you are an adult now with a good-paying job, perhaps you would prefer to find your own place so you can stay here."

"What's the job?"

"Mr. Freeman is opening a new location in Hartshire and has asked me to manage it."

The smile on her father's face warmed her heart. He worked so hard and deserved an opportunity like this. He was one of the best apothecaries among the floating islands. When Sage was little, she often traveled with him when he needed to. As she grew older, her fear of heights manifested, and she struggled to bring herself to go anywhere near the bridges that connected the islands among the clouds.

It was apparent he really wanted to do this, though, and she understood.

"Of course. I understand. When will you be moving?"

His smile faltered. "In a week."

"So soon?!"

"Another manager had been selected but took another job last minute."

"I understand. Congratulations. Really, I'm excited for you. I guess I will start looking for a place tomorrow."

The relieved look on her parents' faces made Sage feel a bit better, but the shock and anxiety of this new development settled in her gut.

She would be fine. Of course, she would. She just needed to find a new place to live in the next week that she could fully cover with her librarian pay.

How hard could that be?

***

Sage stood before one of the most beautiful homes she had ever seen.

The white house with black shutters was the color of freshly fallen snow. Grey slate shingles covered the rooftop, matching the grey stone wall and iron gate surrounding the property. The lawn was perfectly manicured, the bushes cut with a smooth line.

Flower petals from the trees flanking the entryway sprinkled the walkway.

Her parents would move tomorrow, which meant today was the last day to find a place to stay. She quickly learned that her beginner librarian salary didn't go very far when it came to housing in a city as big as Vishneel.

The parchment crumpled slightly in her hand as she steeled her resolve and approached the closed gate. Sage pulled the rope and a melody of bells rang while she waited for someone to let her in.

Soon a butler appeared, with a kind smile. He welcomed Sage onto the grounds, and she followed him through the garden and into the house.

Inside was even more magnificent. Tall ceilings with intricate molding, opulent artwork adorning every wall, and velvet curtains framing dark wood windows. The butler led her to a sitting room in the foyer where she could wait for the lord of the house to arrive.

As she settled into her seat on one of the plush sofas, Sage couldn't help but feel a sense of wonder at being allowed into such a magnificent home.

In the last week, she had seen over twenty places. She wasn't picky, but everywhere she could afford was either too far away from her work, in unsafe areas, or didn't even include a bed. Two were only small corners in the living space of a family home. One had a hole in the roof and looked like it would blow over with a small gust of wind. She scratched the bites on her leg from the flea infestation at the last place she looked at.

"Here to damage more books?"

Sage jumped to her feet and turned toward the doorway.

Prince Finn leaned on the frame, his arms crossed and brow furrowed.

"I wasn't expecting you to be here," Sage said.

"I'm the lord of this house; I can come and go as I please."

Sage flushed, her cheeks burning with embarrassment.

"I should just go. This would never work out. I am so sorry for wasting your time." She made to leave the house, only to find her way blocked by Prince Finn.

"You're here about the position?"

Sage tried to step around him, but he blocked her again.

"Please move."

Finn bent over until his eyes were level with hers.

"I asked you a question."

She glared at him. Shouldn't a prince be more gentlemanly? Who did he think he was keeping her trapped in a house like this?

"I was, but I'm no longer interested."

"Because of me or because you actually aren't interested anymore?"

Sage tried to decide what to do. She had run out of options. This was the last place she had found where she could afford the rent. Really, the room and board were in exchange for working in the house part-time, so it was technically free.

"Never mind that," Finn said.

Sage swallowed nervously.

"I'm sorry, Prince Finn," she said, her eyes downcast. "I made a mistake."

He stared at her for a moment before stepping aside and letting her pass. Sage left the house, eager to escape the prince who had trapped her.

Sage thought about what had just happened as she walked through the city. She couldn't believe that Prince Finn had been so rude.

She had heard stories of his arrogance and cruelty, but she had never honestly thought he was anything like that. Most of the upper class were fae, unlike most of the citizens in the cloud kingdom, Sage included. The fae were more powerful, and while they couldn't outright lie, they were masters of manipulating their words always to benefit themselves, so it made sense that they had worked their way into most of the ruling positions. Perhaps he was just having a bad day, she told herself. Still, she resolved never to speak to him again. She would find a way to live on her own, even if it meant sleeping in a shelter for a few nights until something else opened up.

She refused to be treated poorly by anyone, especially a prince like Finn.

The Gargoyle in the Library

S aying goodbye to her parents had to be the hardest thing she had ever done. Tears streamed down all their faces as they climbed into the wagon, heavily laden with all their belongings.

It took some creative deflecting to convince them that she wanted them to wait to see her new place. She told them it was much too small to take most of her belongings with her, and she wanted to have the chance to make it feel homey before they saw it.

Honestly, she didn't have the heart to tell them that she had no place to stay with them leaving. If she did, she knew they would choose to pass over the promotion, and she could never do that to her father. Not for something he had worked his entire life to achieve.

As long as she avoided Freddy, Sage hoped she could sleep in the library for a few nights while she looked for a new place. Her eyes stung with fresh tears trying to spill over the rims of her eyes as she hid in the cleaning closet of the library. Only a few more minutes and she could leave.

Sitting on the floor of the confined space, her knees pulled to her chest and her head on the wall behind her, Sage allowed her mind to run free.

She had never seen Freddy other than in his stone gargoyle form. A shiver ran down her spine as she imagined what the stone statue must be like while awake and moving. She imagined a gargoyle's steps sounded like rock crumbling, but all of the stones that made up a gargoyle never parted. It was more of a cracking sound as if someone were to pick up a stone or two, set them down, and then pick them up again.

Did his wings and skin stay as stone, or did they turn leathery to the touch like a beast? What about his personality? She really didn't know if gargoyles were more beast or being. Her best guess ... they couldn't actually talk. A mouth full of fangs must make it difficult to do.

Her leg cramping, Sage shifted. Brooms came crashing on top of her.

She froze. Had anyone heard her? Should she run? Did she even have time to?

Heavy footsteps sounded outside the closet.

The door's handle turned, and a large shadow fell over her as it opened. She gasped, finding a man standing there.

"Abandoning your duties so soon?" he asked with a smirk on his handsome face.

The man's eyes were flecked with gold. It wouldn't be noticeable to the naked eye, but to her as an alchemist's daughter who trained with him her entire life, it was as clear as day. The man's eyes glowed as they stared at her.

Messy, chin-length, white hair hung in front of the man's face. A simple linen tunic and brown leather pants covered his surprisingly muscular body. Her nose wrinkled as she noted that he wore no shoes. What kind of person would walk around in a public place without shoes?

"What are you doing?" he asked.

Sage's heart hammered in her chest as she slowly lifted her head. "Just taking a break," she answered a little too quickly.

He walked inside the closet and sat on a bucket. The room was too small for both of them to fit comfortably. He didn't say anything for a long time, and all Sage could do was hold her breath.

"I heard you." His voice was smooth.

Not making eye contact, Sage shook her head. "You heard me what?" she lied.

"I heard you crying," he spoke softly but with a firm tone. "I didn't think it was a good idea to just walk up on you like that, so I was waiting to let you know I was here. When I heard the commotion, I wanted to check on you. You'll have to come out sometime, you know?"

Sage was confused. Who was this stranger to talk to her so comfortably?

She slowly stood, eyeing him cautiously as she gathered her things.

He smiled at her and nodded. "I'm glad you weren't hurt," he said.

Sage couldn't help but smile back at him. She nodded and took a deep breath before rising, trying to compose herself.

Sage felt her heart catch in her throat. The man stood in front of the exit, preventing her from leaving. She stared up into his golden eyes and swallowed hard.

"You know who I am," he said with a grin. "Tell me what my name is."

Struck by fear and confusion, Sage could only shake her head as she tried to walk past him and escape the library before she lost her job. But this man would not allow that to happen so easily.

He reached out his hand, gently touching her arm.

Sage recoiled with a whimper.

Confusion flashed across his face, and with a bow of his head, he stepped aside, allowing her to pass.

Careful not to touch him, she quickly exited into the hall, aiming for the front entrance.

"I'm sorry, Sage. I didn't mean to scare you."

She stopped, turned around, and marched back toward him. "How do you know my name?" she demanded.

The man chuckled and ran his hand through his hair. "I must look completely different during the day. So rarely do I talk to anyone anymore that I sometimes forget that most people I recognize don't know me."

No, it couldn't be! "Freddy?"

His entire face lit up. "That's me."

"But you look so different!"

"I'm guessing I'm not quite this handsome in my other form?"

"Honestly, I don't think you want to know what you actually look like during the day. Let's just say more beast than anything else and keep it at that."

Nodding his head, Freddy kept his eyes on Sage. "Ah, I see."

Sage desperately wanted to ask so many questions. But where to start?!

Freddy smiled and walked past her without saying another word. Confused, she turned around. "Where are you going?"

"The doors are locked, and enchantments to keep robbers out are up. You aren't going anywhere tonight. Let's find a more comfortable place to continue this discussion."

One last glance at the closet she had been hiding in, and she hurried to catch up.

Sage followed Freddy through the library. She assumed he would take her up the stairs and into the restricted section, the area of the library that she had always considered his home, but to her surprise, they walked to the back wall on the first floor.

The flying paper dragon and little reading nooks in the children's section had always made it one of her favorite places in the library. Why Freddy was taking her to this area utterly confused her, though.

She paused at the entrance as he approached the shelves. He reached up to the top shelf, his fingers gripping the spine of one of the books, and he removed it.

Perhaps he was grabbing something to read? The thought made her chuckle. It wasn't the idea of him reading that she found funny. She had already known that he must have had some interest in books. Why else would he work in a library? Specifically choosing a children's book seemed rather far-fetched, though.

Freddy put his hand back up on the shelf's now empty spot, and soon a soft click could be heard. After replacing the book in its home, he grabbed the shelf itself and pushed.

The bookshelf slid back silently.

With a nod of his head, Freddy looked back at her. "Are you coming?"

She didn't know if she should. While comfortable around Freddy, she only knew him as a stone statue.

Sage could hear her mother's voice telling her not to go to strange places with strangers. Especially men. Did she trust him enough to enter a space she didn't know how to escape?

He took a step into the secret hallway behind the shelf.

Freddy turned around, waiting for her.

With a deep breath to calm her nerves, she hesitantly followed him in.

It seemed magical to her, almost like the walls held some sort of secret enchantment, keeping them from closing in on Freddy and her for fear of trapping them. It felt strange to think about it, but it felt true.

The magic surrounding the hall was strong. She could feel it gently brushing against her.

As Freddy turned a corner, Sage saw a small fire illuminating the room.

Shelves and stacks of books from the floor to the ceiling covered the space. No windows could be seen, but in the center sat a small table with two chairs and a trunk beside an oversized plush chair.

"Where are we?" she asked.

"My home. At least the space I can call my own."

"How? This doesn't make any sense. I've walked around the entire library. There's no space that this room could exist in. Are we underground?"

Freddy walked over to the table and poured two glasses of water. "We're not underground. The library has several places like this that were created long ago. Think of it as a magical pocket inside the library. Somewhere to keep the things that need protection the most."

Sage nodded. "So the books with dangerous spells and enchantments on them are here?"

"That's right. It's not just spells, either. Anything our king or head librarian doesn't want people to see or touch is stored here. It's a magical vault that very few people know the existence of or how to access."

Sage couldn't believe she was standing in front of one of the library's secret places.

Books have been her passion since she was a little girl, especially magic books.

She crossed her arms and arched an eyebrow at him. "So why are you showing me then?"

Freddy chuckled as he climbed into the oversized chair.

"Because someone decided to be a stowaway. If it were anyone else, I would have kicked them out before the library was sealed. You, though," he swirled the water in his glass before continuing, "have earned at least a bit of my trust. I assumed if you were hiding in the library, you must have a good reason."

Sage looked at the fire. She walked to the table, picked up the glass he had poured earlier, and took a sip, avoiding his gaze.

She lowered the glass. "I have nowhere else to go," she mumbled.

"Why is that?"

She pulled out the chair and slumped into it, dropping her small bag of belongings on the floor beside it. "My parents moved, and I didn't have the heart to tell them I couldn't find anywhere to stay before they left. I tried... No, I *am trying* to find somewhere. It's just been much harder to do than I expected it to be."

Freddy stood from his chair and joined her at the table. He placed his large hand on hers. The heat from his hand made her gasp. "You can stay here if you want to for a few days. Not permanently, but I'll give you a month to find somewhere else to go."

Tears began to well in her eyes. "Thank you," she whispered.

"Don't thank me yet. I won't kick you out, but it may become an issue if anyone else finds out you are staying here. Besides," he gestured around him, "I don't have the most comfortable arrangement for non-gargoyle guests."

She smiled and sighed in relief. "It's better than the street. Truly, I'm most grateful."

***

"What have you done to my kitchen?"

At the sound of Piper's voice, Sage spun around, knocking her steamed milk from the wooden counter onto the floor. "Whoops." She giggled.

"Sage," Piper scowled, "why are you trying to make coffee in my kitchen? You're a terrible cook, and I would rather you not burn down the coffee shop."

"Oh, I'm not that bad."

Piper's raised brow said she thought otherwise. "This coming from the girl who can't cook scrambled eggs. You literally just stir it until it isn't a liquid anymore. The last thing we need is one of your accidents and this whole place to burn down."

Sage mocked a gasp., "Not my books! You play dirty. It's not my fault the eggs always taste like dragon breath."

Grabbing a towel, Piper tossed it at her friend. "Technically, it is. You get distracted, and over-cooked eggs taste like sulfur. Clean up your mess, and I can make you a drink. What are you doing here so early anyway?"

The towel slipped from Sage's fingers, and she dropped to her knees to catch it. She began wiping up the mess while avoiding her friend's eyes. She was never very good at lying.

"I wanted to get a head start on the new book shipment. Get them on the shelves as fast as possible." An idea struck her. "Would you be willing to teach me how to make coffee? It wouldn't have to be anything fancy, but something simple to make when I'm here early. My new place doesn't have anywhere I can make it myself."

"Oh," Piper squatted and touched Sage's hand. "I forgot your parents left. Of course. How are you holding up?"

Sage rose and placed the towel on the counter. "I'm alright. It's about time I was on my own anyway. Now, where do we start?"

Piper placed a metal and wood object on the counter. A small metal dome with a tiny door sat above a wooden box. Wheels and bars connected and turned to meet a wheel with a small handle on the side.

The smell of coffee hit Sage's nose as Piper lifted the lid on a white glass jar.

As Piper handed Sage a small scoop, she pointed from the jar to the contraption sitting on the counter.

"Open the little door on the coffee grinder and put three scoops of these coffee beans into it. Only use this jar, though. The others are different types of coffee beans for drinks other than what I am teaching you."

Sage placed the coffee in the coffee grinder and closed the small door.

"Now turn the handle until you feel the resistance ease up."

Crunching sounds came from the machine as Sage slowly turned the handle. She flinched and eyed her friend, looking for reassurance that she wasn't just breaking this machine. After a few moments, she could feel the change and the sound began to ease up.

"Well done. As much as I know you love your lattes, you cannot be trusted with our espresso machine. Your magic is too low to control the stones that power it, and the last thing we need is for you to blow up the library."

"Again, you and your threatening of my beloved books."

The two laughed.

"Now, open the stove door and turn the knob to high. It can also be run using the stones, but the stove has a regulator, so even you shouldn't be able to mess it up," Piper said with a wink.

Piper filled a small kettle with water and placed it on the burner. She then turned on another burner and put a small pan with milk in it.

Soon the kettle whistled, and Piper pulled it off. She handed Sage a thermometer. "Watch for when the temperature drops to two hundred while I get the press."

Piper added the freshly ground coffee and hot water to a clear glass press and left it to sit for several minutes. Sage observed her friend expertly move from one task to another, adding ingredients or adjusting heat levels with ease. Her own hands shook with excitement at being able to learn such an intricate process.

Soon, the familiar scent of coffee filled the air, along with the sweet aroma of vanilla, lavender, and frothy milk. Sage breathed deeply, savoring every moment of this newfound skill she had learned from her best friend.

Together, the two sat at one of the library's tables, sipping their delicious coffee and chatting happily.

"Well, what do you think?" Piper asked, smiling. "It's perfect. Thank you."

"Of course! What are friends for?"

Taking another sip, Sage smiled back, already planning on making a cup for Freddy tonight. She was determined to put the skills she had learned today to good use and show her new roommate how much she appreciated his help.

***

With two cups of hot coffee, Sage stood in front of the bookshelf in the children's section. Why hadn't she asked Freddy how to open this secret door?

While setting the drinks on a shelf, Sage looked for something to boost herself enough to see the top of the shelf itself. A wooden chair caught her eye. She dragged the heavy piece of furniture across the floor. The legs shrieked in protest against the smooth wood and raised puffs of dust. Making a mental note to do a deep clean of this section of the library tomorrow, Sage placed the back of the chair against the bookshelf.

She climbed onto it, gripping the shelf to steady herself. Gingerly, she reached up and ran her fingers along the books' spines. Estimating where she had seen him pull the book from the night before, she began pulling the books out one by one, holding them in the crook of her elbow.

Just as she was about to give up, her fingers brushed against something cold and metallic.

Sage smiled as with a small push the secret door was revealed. Stepping down from the chair, she returned it to its home and grabbed the two cups of coffee from the shelf. She sipped her coffee, humming happily as she climbed into the hidden compartment behind the bookshelf.

She saw a small chest sitting on the floor as she entered her temporary home. It wasn't there the night before. Excitedly, she rushed over and lifted the lid, only to find it empty.

Baffled, Sage frowned down at the chest. What could have been in the trunk if this secret space was empty?

She heard footsteps sounding from outside the door. She quickly shut the chest and ducked behind one of the stacks of books, holding her breath as she listened intently.

Her heart pounding in her chest, she heard someone fumbling with the secret door's lock. It slowly creaked open, and soon Freddy's face appeared.

"Hi," he said, smiling at her.

"Hi." She grinned back. "You're just in time for coffee."

Freddy stepped into the secret space and set a plate of bread and cheese on the small table. He walked over to the fireplace and lit a fire, sending sparks of gold dancing around the room.

Sage watched in wonder as he created a cozy little nook in the hidden space.

"Can I ask you a question?"

Freddy took the cup of coffee from her outstretched hand. "Of course."

"How much magic can gargoyles do? I know you use magic to check out books in the library; apparently, you can use fire magic. Do you have limits or specialties like mages do?"

He shook his head and moved to sit in the plush chair near the fire.

"What do you know about gargoyles?"

She thought for a moment before answering. "Not much. Just that at night, you're alive and apparently fae. During the day, you are a stone statue."

He swirled the cup and took a slow sip. "Technically, I'm still alive in my stone form. Have you ever seen any gargoyles other than myself?"

Sage shook her head no.

"Gargoyles are the end game for cursed fae, Sage."

Sage nearly dropped the cup but splashed the hot liquid on her hand instead. She hurried to place it on the table and wipe the burning drink from her tender skin.

A deep laugh erupted from Freddy.

"You're joking."

Wiping tears, he took a deep breath, set his coffee cup down beside him, and leaned forward.

"I would never joke about something like this," he said in a severe tone, his gold-flecked eyes piercing. "We are mages."

She was baffled by this. She didn't understand why any mage would willingly become a stone statue. The books always told stories of how the stone statues had lived long happy lives, but was it all a lie? Maybe they didn't know. Mages could do anything with a single thought. Why would they choose to become stone beings?

"So, all gargoyles are mages?"

He nodded. "Gargoyles are some of the most powerful mages in existence. We can do just about anything with our magic. The only reason you haven't seen any other gargoyles is that once it sets in, we tend to retreat. We become vulnerable. It is irreversible once it begins. It's something that no one chooses. More often than not, it's forced on us by circumstance."

Sage sat opposite him, her mind spinning with questions.

"How many of you are there?"

"I don't know. The king doesn't want the general population to know that the most powerful have such a weakness. Our magic is so powerful that it eventually destroys our fae form. Once the curse takes hold, we tend to hide. We turn to stone and stay that way until our magic fades away completely."

"So, you're saying all mages will turn to stone eventually?"

"Not all mages. It only happens when a mage does magic beyond their natural capability."

Sage felt saddened by this. "You're sure there's no way to reverse it? How does a mage know when they are beginning to turn?"

"There's no cure. If you stop early enough and limit your magic use, you can prevent yourself from turning fully into a gargoyle. You just feel aged and as if you have achy bones. Your fingernails become grey during the day, and slowly, more areas show signs of turning to stone."

"Is your work in the library killing you faster?"

Freddy nodded, his face somber. "It's only a matter of time."

"Why do you do it then?"

With a small, tired smile, he leaned back in his chair and gestured around the hidden room. "A favor to the crown and a quiet life reading books for the end of my days. It's really a great way to go."

Sage was having trouble comprehending it all. She couldn't imagine being bound to a stone existence. And yet, she could understand why Freddy was willing to live out the end of his stone existence like this. He had books. One of the things Sage loved most in the world. If she were going to turn to stone eventually, she would want to be in a library until the end.

"If you don't mind me asking, how long have you been a gargoyle?"

"Almost three hundred years."

"Excuse me?! How is that even possible?"

"All part of the curse."

"What made you turn?"

He chuckled. "Now, that, I'm not willing to share. It's a secret that isn't entirely mine to tell."

Sage swallowed. "How much time do you have left?"

"I don't know. Not long. My time as a fae is growing shorter and shorter."

"Does it make you sad?"

"I said my goodbyes long ago."

She noted how he avoided giving a direct answer to her question. Sage's magic was weak, but she was brilliant. She had grown up learning everything she could and knew the skills of an apothecary.

Picking up a slice of bread and a chunk of cheese, she looked at Freddy as if she were seeing him for the first time. An idea formed in her mind that she didn't dare speak out loud but one that she was willing to devote her life to.

She would figure out a way to reverse this curse.

Something's Wrong With the Prince

S age stood in the library, marveling at the small group of wide-eyed children fidgeting excitedly around her.

"Welcome to story time," she said, grinning. "Who is ready to learn about dragons?"

The children gazed up at her in wonder, their eyes shining with excitement as they waited eagerly for Sage to begin.

Sage smiled and took a deep breath, her heart racing with anticipation as she began to weave a magical story filled with wondrous details and captivating legends about those fierce and powerful beasts.

She told them of dragons larger than houses, with wingspans wider than the village's circumference. Dragons that circled the village and breathed fire into every corner and crevice, leaving behind melted rock, smoke, and soot. Their razor-sharp claws, scales that glimmered like polished jewels in the sunlight, and their wings that sliced through the air so fast they were a blur.

The children's eyes were wide, and they gasped in wonder as she spun the tale of how their ancestors had defeated those great beasts.

Nearing the end of the story, Sage stood and held her arms out as if they were wings. "These magnificent creatures could breathe fire hotter than any furnace," she said calmly, walking among the children, "destroying everything in their path with terrifying strength. The human armies stood no chance against such powerful creatures. Not until our kingdom, Sarash, created mage guilds and organized the most powerful weapons we have.

"A grand battle deep in the Rolling Mountains waged for weeks until finally, our mages came out victorious. Not a single human or fae soul was lost, and no dragons were left."

"That's not entirely true." A deep voice interrupted her. "Many mages were lost. They just died after the battle was over."

Sage spun to face the man who dared to correct her.

Prince Finn stood at the entrance to the children's section, his shaggy hair hanging in his black eyes. A frown cut lines over his forehead and around his mouth. Beside him stood a man with familiar violet eyes and a confident grin. Had Piper said his name was Colby? Maybe?

Sage glared at them, the children's faces growing solemn with the mood change. "You know nothing of the events that transpired during the battle."

"I do," Prince Finn said, turning to address the children and parents present. "As Librarian Sage said, the battle lasted for weeks. During this time, many mages grew very sick from using so much magic. They died shortly after the battle was over."

Several children gasped and whimpered as they went to find their parents, their faces tear-streaked, lips quivering.

Sage's fists clenched as she tried to calm her frustration. "Prince Finn," she said through a tight smile, "I appreciate the history lesson, but this is a *children's* story-time hour. Is there anything I can help you with?"

Colby cleared his throat, directing her attention back to him. "I need a few minutes of your time."

She stared at him, waiting for him to continue.

"Alone, please."

Taking a slow breath, she excused herself and escorted Prince Finn and Colby to a more private aisle nearby.

"How can I help you? I only have a moment."

Prince Finn eyed her. "You could tell the truth and not pretend that everyone came out of the battle unscathed," he said.

"I *am* telling the truth. As I said, no one died *during* the battle. The deaths after could have been attributed to other things as well."

Dark brown eyes glared at her through the prince's shaggy hair. "I could have been more honest if that would have made you happy. I could have shared how they didn't die as a result of the battle but as a result of their weakness. They weren't fit to be mages, and they knew it."

"That is an incredibly callous thing to say," she spat while trying to keep her voice quiet enough for the library. "Those mages didn't ask to be born with magic in their blood. They were all talented mages who dedicated their lives to end the suffering our people endured from the dragons. You have no right to judge them like that."

Sage stared down the prince with growing anger. She despised him for his callous indifference to the sacrifices those mages had made.

"I judge them for their actions, not for what lies in their blood," he said flatly.

"What are you talking about? I'm going to have you escorted out before—"

The prince scoffed. "Before, what? No one is going to do anything to me, Sage. My family literally owns this library. I could easily have you fired for your insubordination if I wished."

He looked smug, and she wanted to slap him. He wasn't wrong, though. Even if he weren't fae and could lie to her, he was part of the family she technically worked for.

"What are you *really* doing here, Prince Finn?" she snapped

Colby pulled a large leather book from under his arm and held it out. "We came to return this."

"You return books at the front desk." Sage's eyes darted to Prince Finn. "As you so kindly pointed out, this is *literally* your library. You, of all people, should know that."

"True," Colby said, causing Sage's eyes to waver from Prince Finn, "but since we didn't check it out officially, we thought it best to give it back to the librarian who saw us leave with it."

"I understand why you came here, but I wonder why both of you had to return the book together. Afraid the little librarian would attack you again?"

Prince Finn rolled his eyes. "He may have carried it out of the library, but I carried it out of the restricted section. Besides, I wanted to talk to you. You intrigue me."

She couldn't have heard him right. This was only the second time she had met this man, and the last time, they had only seen each other for a moment.

"You could have just asked me to join you for some tea. And I would have told you that I'm busy."

The prince let out an unamused chuckle. "Tea? My mother always said that tea is to be shared with friends, and I don't believe I know anyone here who would qualify as such."

With amusement, Colby's head swiveled between them as they argued, the book tucked back under his arm.

"On that, you are correct. It seems you really didn't need to make this trip to see me specifically. The return desk is that way," she said, pointing toward the entrance with a pasted-on simile. "We don't care who returns the books as long as they are indeed returned." She offered a slight bow and walked away from the prince. "Have a good day, Your Highness."

It took everything in her to walk and not run back to the children's section. She intrigued him? That was highly doubtful, but she wasn't willing to stick around long enough to find out if it was true.

***

Sage pulled her cloak tighter as she hurried alongside Freddy in the dark alley. "Are we almost there?"

With a cock of his head, he grinned. A twinkle in his eye told her he was up to something, but she couldn't figure out what.

"Somehow, I imagined that you never left the library. Do you usually leave the library?"

"Not usually. Only when there's somewhere I want to be or something I need."

Sage waited for him to continue, but he never did. The last hour had been unexpected, to say the least.

Freddy had approached her as she was closing the library for the night. He told her that he had something to show her, and, of course, she was intrigued.

In the back corner of his private library, behind a bookshelf, was the secret tunnel's entrance.

Of course, he had a secret tunnel in his secret room. Why hadn't she expected that? Hadn't he told her the night he found her that there was no other way out? How had he gotten around lying about that? He was fae, after all. Not that she minded. She would take sleeping in the library over the streets any day.

Sage had been hesitant, but Freddy assured her that the spells protecting the library would keep everything secure and that this tunnel changed its exit location every time someone used it, so no one could break in that way. So she agreed to go with him, and now there they were, hurrying through a dark alley toward who knew what.

Eventually, they stopped in front of a large stone wall. There was nothing special about it, but Freddy seemed to know what he was doing. He muttered something under his breath and waved his hand over the wall's surface. A thin door materialized, just big enough for them to squeeze through one at a time.

"After you," he said, gesturing for her to go first.

Sage took a deep breath and stepped through the door, quickly followed by Freddy. The hallway was dark and narrow, but it opened into a large room with no windows that seemed to sink into the ground.

People were hurrying toward the arena in the middle, eager to get a good seat for whatever spectacle they would be witnessing.

Sage was swept up in the excitement of it all and couldn't help but wonder what they had come here to see. Whatever it was, she knew she would enjoy every minute of it.

"What is this place?"

"Welcome to the Underground. Have you ever been to one of Sarash's mage rankings?"

"Never."

"You're in for a treat."

Freddy threaded through the crowd down a steep flight of stairs, Sage close behind in his wake. Clusters of people stood around, talking and people-watching as they waited for the event to start. Freddy zeroed in on two empty seats near the front of the stage and led Sage over to them. A drop of almost three men high separated the tiers of seats from the stage below. Only a wooden railing to prevent the audience from joining the impending fights below.

"Any mage guild wanting to take on official quests must participate in the battles yearly. The higher you rank, the more difficult and better-paying jobs you can take. They are brutal, entertaining, and often deadly. This," Freddy gestured to the arena, "is where the guilds that don't qualify to join the main battles compete. Some tamper in darker magic, while others refuse to work for the kingdom. Tonight is different, though."

Sage kept a close eye on the empty arena while Freddy talked, afraid she would miss the start of whatever was happening tonight. "How is this different?"

"One of the dark guilds challenged the top guild in the kingdom. Usually, they wouldn't accept the challenge, and no one knows why they did. Which is why tonight has such a good turnout."

"Wait, the Charming Four will fight down there against a dark guild?"

Freddy burst out laughing. "I didn't have you pegged for one of those girls. Please, tell me you call them that to their faces."

"Of course not! At this point, everyone calls them that."

The look in his eye made Sage squirm. Freddy chuckled. "I suppose it's their fault for not choosing a name when they formed their guild. I feel the name has served them well, don't you?"

Sage could feel her cheeks burning as she avoided Freddy's smiling face.

"So they are here to fight a dark guild. Shouldn't that mean they are at an advantage, being the top guild in the kingdom?"

"Not necessarily. They are only the top out of the official guilds. Even in an unofficial match they still have to follow rules or it could hurt their reputation. A dark mage could do anything."

Sage looked out at the crowd again. Apprehension began to fill her about the night to come.

"Don't worry." Freddy pointed to several etchings on the railing. "We won't be hurt. They've put in a barrier so physical attacks can't get to the crowd. Of course, there are a few things that can't stop, but there's never been an injury to the crowd at one of these events."

The crowd's voices' low murmur reverberated off the coliseum's marble walls. A thick fog rolled over the arena, swallowing the stone benches where the crowd sat. It swept over them, leaving them invisible, and then dissipated as quickly as it came.

Four figures walked out into the arena's center, causing the crowd to erupt in cheers. The Charming Four had arrived.

Sage's heart beat faster as they strode around the arena floor. They were easily over six feet tall, and their physiques were impressive like they had been sculpted by a master artist. Their movements were graceful and confident, and Sage could feel the excitement building in the crowd as all eyes remained on them.

The Charming Four walked with purpose, clearly ready for battle.

Sage noticed, too, that the Charming Four equally enthralled the crowd. There was something special about them, something that drew people in and made them worship at their feet.

And then she saw the dark mages.

The dark mages were a group of five, three men and two women. They walked with an air of confidence as intoxicating as the Charming Four's. They wore all black, their clothes clinging to their bodies like oil on water. Sage could feel the power emanating from their piercing eyes from where she sat.

The two groups faced off against each other, the tension in the air thickening. It was electric like a storm was brewing. Her heart raced, and she leaned forward in her seat, eager to see what would happen next.

Without any announcement, the dark mages attacked. They moved with such speed and agility that Sage could barely follow what was happening.

The Charming Four circled up, each man facing out. Ice slowly crept across the arena floor as a mound rose around the four, blocking them from the dark mages' view. The mound was covered in such a thick layer of ice that it would be impossible to climb it to attack.

The dark mages threw spell after spell at the Charming Four, and Sage could see the looks of concentration on their faces as they deflected the attacks. Ice and soil refilled the affected areas almost immediately.

The crowd was on their feet now, cheering and jeering for both sides. The excitement coursed through her veins, and she found herself rooting for the Charming Four even though she didn't know them.

The Charming Four seemed to be waiting for something, and then Sage saw Colby raise his hands and a thick thorny vine of ice rose from the ground beside him. Sage noticed a tiny change in the ice below Sawyer moving to their right. The soil in a section of the mound dropped, the ice left behind creating a crystal clear window, and the vine shattered the ice, sending itself surrounded by shards at one of the men of the dark guild.

Sage wondered how the Charming Four were coordinating their attacks. While the dark guild couldn't see into the protected barrier to attack, she assumed the Charming Four couldn't see out of it either while the mound was both dirt and ice.

The man could dodge most of it, but a few slivers caught his arm, causing him to drop to his knees. He summoned a shield made of darkness just in time to block a fireball from Prince Finn.

Some of the other dark mages took this opportunity to charge while the wall was down.

The vine arched up and quickly swung like a whip at the two women. Screams echoed in the arena from the women and the dark guild's fans as it hit the women in the chest.

With a roar, the tallest dark mage, his eyes almost black, charged the mound's opening. Electricity gathered around him.

The ground rose, shattering the thorny vine and filling in the gap, instantly covering it in a thick sheet of ice once again.

It was becoming clear that the Charming Four and the dark mages were evenly matched. The fight raged on, and neither side seemed to be gaining an advantage. Sage could see the looks of determination on both sides and found herself holding her breath.

Asher seemed to be controlling the earth beneath him, moving it to trip their enemies or shield himself from their attacks. Seeing an opening, Colby used his powers to create another thick ice vine, which lashed out at one of the dark mages, shattering his shield and causing him to drop to his knees.

As the battle continued, the Charming Four started to gain an edge. The four mages worked together seamlessly, using their talents to counter and outmaneuver the dark guild members.

She started to suspect that when the group was tucking within their mound and were unable to see, Sawyer was directing the group. Small changes in the ice below his feet always happened just before they attacked, almost as if he was sending and receiving signals from his ice that covered the arena. There were only slight changes. Sometimes the ice became clouded, others it looked as if a reflection of light flashed across the surface, but it always happened just before the guild made a move. Sage had to admit, they were impressive in a fight.

With a roar, Colby sent a blast of wind and ice at one of the dark mages, knocking him to the ground.

Prince Finn took this opportunity to launch a firewall at another enemy, while Sawyer used his earth magic to create a wall of spikes and trap a third dark mage.

They worked together to systematically destroy their opponents, turning the tide and leaving the dark mages reeling.

As the crowd's energy shifted, her excitement grew, knowing it was only a matter of time before the Charming Four defeated the dark mages. She cheered along with the rest of the crowd, urging the Charming Four to victory.

The two female dark mages leaped into the air and fired black smoke at the Charming Four.

Sawyer threw a dome of ice over them to block it, but it was too late. The smoke expanded within the enclosed space.

It was pitch black.

No one in the crowd could see anything.

The light from Prince Finn's flames suddenly filled the dome, instantly melting the ice and evaporating the black magic. Fire rolled over the mound and filled the arena before disappearing.

Shock seemed to fill the room, everyone sitting in silence, before the crowd erupted into cheers.

Every member of the dark guild lay on the ground unconscious.

When Sage looked at the Charming Four her excitement at their victory was dampened. Prince Finn was unconscious and Asher and Sawyer were carrying him out of the arena.

Freddy nudged her. "Let's go. I need to help them."

Sage followed Freddy down some stairs, leading them to a set of hallways. They entered a room and Sage closed the door behind them. Prince Finn lie on a bed with the rest of his team surrounding him.

"He hasn't woken up?" Freddy asked as he hurried to check Prince Finn.

"Not yet," Asher said, glancing from Freddy to Sage."What's wrong with him?" Sage asked, worry etched into her voice.

"He overexerted himself casting that last spell," Freddy replied, gently prodding at Finn's arm. "He needs to rest and heal for a few days before he's back to full strength."

Freddy's eyes held concern because he understood the consequences of that kind of action better than most.

She looked around the room, watching as Sawyer and Asher carefully tended to the cut on Finn's cheek. Colby was standing by the door, his brow furrowed in worry.

"How can we help him?" Sage asked.

"This is probably hard for you to understand," Freddie said, looking over at Sage, "but you must trust us. You can't do anything to help him. All you can do is wait."

Sage hesitated for a second. As much as she found Finn to be a pain in her side, she didn't like seeing anyone hurt. She wasn't sure she could accept that.

"I'm going to get something to help replenish Prince Finn," Freddy said as he motioned for Asher to follow him.

Sage was left alone with Sawyer and Colby, who watched her while they waited for the other two to return. Both looked worn and tired with dark rings under their eyes. Much of Sawyer's red hair had escaped from the tie that had held it back during the fight while Colby's cropped blond hair was slick with sweat. While their appearances were disheveled, there were no physical wounds that Sage could see which would need tending. Choosing to ignore them, she moved over to Prince Finn's side to take a closer look. For the most part, he looked to be peacefully sleeping, but she noticed his fingernails appeared slightly grey.

She held out her hands in front of her to compare. There was definitely a slight difference.

"What are you doing?"

Prince Finn's voice made her jump.

"Freddy and Asher will be right back," she said.

"I didn't ask what they were doing, did I?"

He pulled himself to a sitting position on the bed, his eyes glittering with an intensity that made her feel like he could see right through her.

"*What* are you doing?" he asked again.

Asher reentered the room. "How are you feeling?"

"What is she doing here?"

Freddy carried in a flask and a pouch. "She came with me."

"*Why?*" Finn asked. His tone was sharp and commanding, and it caused a shiver to run down Sage's back.

"Where are my manners?" Freddy asked. "Prince Finn, this is Sage. My temporary roommate."

Colby approached them with a glint in his eye. "Roommate, huh? Didn't realize you had gotten a girlfriend, Fredrick."

Sawyer smirked as he took the pouch from Freddy and opened it. "Did our gargoyle get a pet?"

Freddy shot him a dirty look. "She's not a pet."

"Whatever you say." Colby winked.

"Girlfriend, huh?" Sawyer's smirk never left. "That's some pretty fast dating, Fredrick."

"Shut up," Sage mumbled. "I'm looking for a place to stay."

"Still haven't found anywhere? I was sure you had somewhere to go after you stormed out of our place," Prince Finn replied.

Sage shot Prince Finn a glare.

"That was you? Finn here was so worked up the rest of the day. So much so that he—" Colby's voice cut off when the back of Prince Finn's hand smacked into his stomach.

"I was fine. I *am* fine. Let's get out of here."

Prince Finn attempted to stand, only to find Freddy pushing him back onto the bed.

"Not before you take this."

Sawyer handed Freddy several things from the pouch to put in the flask. The prince rolled his eyes and held out his hand, waiting.

"Did you ... ?" Sage whispered before stopping herself.

Asher offered her a small encouraging smile. "What did you need?"

"Nothing. I just... Never mind."

The rest of the group turned their attention to her. "Yes?" Freddy asked.

"Did you get ginger and drasken mushroom?"

"No, why?" Sawyer replied.

"His fingernails," she said, pointing at Prince Finn. "They're discolored. Ginger will help with the inflammation from overuse, and the drasken mushroom helps regenerate the body. It may help counter some of the effects before they fully set in."

Freddy's eyes widened while the others just stared at her.

"How do you know this?" the prince asked.

"My father is an apothecary. I practically grew up in the shop he worked in."

"But you became a librarian?" Asher asked.

She shrugged. "I love books."

Freddy cleared his throat and held the flask out to Sawyer. "You heard her. Add it."

"You're sure?" Sawyer asked.

"Look at him. I can't believe I didn't notice the discoloration myself. It's worth a try."

Sawyer dug into the pouch filled with small envelopes and bottles, looking for the ingredients.

Something itched at the back of Sage's mind as she watched the group. "How do you all know Freddy?"

"We grew up with him," Asher responded. "When we were small, he wasn't stuck in the library as much. He taught us some and was occasionally part of the court before the curse progressed."

"We're lucky to have him," Colby added.

"Will you just hurry up and give me the potion? I want to get out of here," Prince Finn grumped.

Freddy shook the flask one last time and opened it before handing it to the prince. "You know, it sounds like there's a simple solution to all your problems right now. Sage needs somewhere to stay, and you lot need someone who knows at least the basics about medical stuff. I'm awake less and less and won't always be here to help you out."

"They've got me," Sawyer argued.

"They do, but I bet she knows much more than you do."

Suddenly five pairs of eyes were focused on her, making her squirm.

"I think it's a good idea." Asher was the first to speak. "I promise no matter what our reputation may be, we will be nothing but honorable toward you if you live with us. The room and food would be free. You could still work in the library but need to travel with us on some of our jobs."

"That's right. It can be like you're the princess of the group," Freddie finished.

She cringed at the thought. "I don't want to be the princess of anything."

"Then what's the problem?"

She looked at Prince Finn and then back at the rest of the group in front of her.

"I guess there isn't one."

Dinner with the Charming Four

S age stood in her new bedroom. White walls contrasted with the wood ceiling and furniture. Dust danced in the light that shone through a large window and delicately landed on the dresser below it. The view from the second floor was stunning. The manicured garden and stone walls made her feel as if she were no longer inside the city, even though she was in the center of it.

Her meager bag of personal belongings sat on the small bed, and a familiar trunk was positioned at the foot. She opened the lid to find a pile of packages wrapped in brown paper and tied with string, filling it to the brim, with a small note on top.

A little something to get you started. I assume most of your belongings went with your parents, so I gathered a few items to help you with your new home. If they get too rowdy, send them my way.

-Your now ex-roommate, Freddy

Sage smiled as she clasped the note to her chest, feeling a warm rush of gratitude for her friend. She eagerly unwrapped the packages, revealing beautiful clothing, artful decorations, and a bright emerald-green bedding set.

Asher entered the room and saw Sage gazing in amazement at the gifts. He grinned at her.

"What do you think of your room?" he asked eagerly.

"It's beautiful."

"I'm glad you think so. Dinner is ready if you would like to join us."

Sage looked down at herself. She had been in such a hurry to get to the house she hadn't even changed clothes. She still wore her work clothes, now covered in grime from an old box of books she had discovered hidden away. She blushed as she thought about it.

"I should go change," she said.

"I will wait for you outside."

Asher gently closed the door behind him. Sage picked out a simple red dress and, with a glance in the mirror to ensure she was put together, she opened the door to find Asher leaning on the opposite wall.

"Shall we?" he asked.

Sage smiled and nodded, before walking out of the room and down the stairs toward the dining room. The other three were already sitting at the table, chatting excitedly about something. They stopped talking as Sage entered, their eyes landing on her.

"You look lovely." Colby smiled.

"Thanks," Sage replied shyly, sitting beside him.

The talk resumed as a plate of food was placed before Sage. A pile of mashed potatoes with a perfect bowl of gravy made from the roast sitting inside it, a slice of roast, and a larger variety of vegetables than she had ever seen on one plate. It looked delicious.

A basket of warm bread and butter sat in the center of the table. Sage helped herself to a slice and dipped it into the mashed potatoes and gravy, breaking the dam that held it in place. She made a happy hum as she took her first bite and the gravy ran down the potatoes onto the roast.

"You know, we probably would have won if someone didn't pass out."

Suddenly tuned into the conversation, Sage looked at Sawyer. If her mouth weren't full of food, it would have been wide open.

"If I remember correctly," Prince Finn said, spinning a goblet, "we did win, thanks to me."

Sawyer scoffed. "Does it really count as winning if you freaked out from the dark and threw a spell before passing out?"

With a shrug, Prince Finn took a sip of his drink. "A win is a win."

"We wouldn't have had to fight if someone hadn't been flirting with one of the dark guild's girls," Colby said.

Sawyer choked on a bite of mashed potatoes. "Look who's talking. I wasn't the only one involved in that."

Sage chuckled, resulting in four pairs of eyes suddenly on her. She froze.

With a smirk, Colby cocked his head. "You find that funny?"

Swallowing her bite, she hesitated. "Honestly, yeah. I do. I wondered how they had roped you into fighting them. It didn't exactly appear to be your scene."

"What would you consider our scene?" Asher asked.

Sage paused in thought before gesturing around the room. "This. I would assume four rich and powerful men who live in a place like this stayed a bit more above board. Especially when one of them is a prince."

Sawyer leaned forward, his fork outstretched and pointing at her. "Do you know why we live together here instead of in our family homes?"

"I assumed because you formed a guild. Don't guilds normally do that sort of thing?"

He laughed. "Guilds normally don't have guys like us. We formed the guild to have somewhere away from the noble pressure. Have a way to escape when needed and to indulge in our darker and less pristine interests."

Sage had no desire to discover those darker interests at this time, so she kept her mouth shut and only nodded.

Asher grinned at her. "Most noble men and women our age have to marry their own kind, or they fall out of grace and lose everything. We, on the other hand, do not. We can do as we please. None of us are first sons and we won't inherit our families' fortunes or responsibilities. No need to marry some noble girl we wouldn't want to be around for more than a few seconds."

Sage chewed her lip for a moment, not liking where this conversation was heading. "So why do you stay in the capital then?"

Prince Finn cleared his throat. "Because we have a mission to fulfill, and being a guild allows us access to the resources we need to do it. Other guilds would beat us to those resources if we lived outside the capital."

"That's where you come in, Sage," Colby added. "We've been looking for someone to help treat injuries without notifying our families. Something that the four of us have difficulty with, given our notoriety. Maybe even fill in as cook sometimes on our missions."

Sage burst out laughing. "You don't want me doing that. I'm a terrible cook."

"But you do know how to follow a recipe, right? How could you be a bad cook when you were trained as an apothecary?" Prince Finn asked.

"Have you ever had anything from an apothecary that tasted good?"

The four had thoughtful looks before they shook their heads no.

"Exactly. Sorry, I'm the last person you want preparing your meals. I can keep you alive, but I can't make them taste good. Can I ask a question, though?"

"Of course," Colby responded.

"What's this mission you're working on?"

Prince Finn placed his goblet on the table with a *thunk.* "That's not something we can divulge at this time. Just know that we will give you any information you need as you need it."

She nodded and turned her attention back to her plate. Somehow, she felt she was in trouble, and she wasn't sure why.

***

Sage walked to the apothecary her father had worked in, deep in thought.

The conversation from dinner the night before was still fresh in her mind. Had she stumbled on something she wasn't meant to know? She was no stranger to danger, as she had seen it often enough as an apothecary's daughter. Helping him care for the sickest of patients, some she assumed were on the run from someone. But this felt different somehow, and a chill ran down her spine.

As she entered the familiar shop, Sage saw Will tending to customers behind the counter. His freshly cut sandy hair made his already sharp features appear even more so. If they hadn't been friends since childhood she would almost think he was handsome, but there was too much history there for Sage to consider that.

He smiled warmly and waved her over.

"What brings you here today?" he said in a friendly greeting. "I feel like I haven't seen you in forever." He leaned against the counter.

She ran her fingers along some of the canisters lining the shelves, pausing as memories of watching her father work came flooding back.

Sage cleared her throat. "I was thinking of getting some ingredients for some remedies I'm making," she replied slowly, not wanting to give away too much information.

A look of concern spread across his face. "Are you sick? You've got to be taking better care of yourself. Especially with your parents gone."

"I'm fine. It's for a part-time job I picked up. Something to help cover the cost of room and board. It's just a few remedies. Nothing serious."

He stared at her, perhaps looking for any signs of illness. Satisfied, he took her list, turned, and started gathering the ingredients.

"When do I get to come to see your new place? You've been so secretive about it," Will said as he placed jars and herbs on the counter.

Unease settled in her gut. She couldn't let him see where she was staying. Will was incredibly protective of her, and if he knew she was living with the Charming Four, his reaction would be about as bad as she imagined her parents would be.

"I'd love to have you over sometime. I don't have much furniture yet, but I'll be getting some soon."

Will smiled. "That's fine. I've done a lot of camping, so I'm more than happy to sit on the floor."

He laughed when she playfully punched his arm.

"Look, why don't you admire the new glass jars we just got in? I know you have a soft spot for the blues," he said suddenly with a nod. "I'll finish up here and have your ingredients ready for you by the time you're done."

Will's encouraging smile was enough to make her relax. His feelings for her went beyond friendship, but she didn't feel the same way. She nodded gratefully as she moved toward the shelf he had mentioned.

Beautiful clear, blue, and green glass bottles and jars of varying sizes and shapes, each topped with a cork or wooden lid, filled the shelf. Sage examined them carefully, admiring the intricate detail on each jar while her mind wandered back to thoughts of the Charming Four. An idea formed in her mind.

She had already planned on billing all of the items she was purchasing to the guild, even though they had yet to show her a prepped space for her to store her ingredients. A space had been promised and they couldn't expect her to pay for stocking it, could they? Suffice it to say, she shouldn't feel bad about grabbing containers to store them in as well.

The fresh smell of rain mingled with the sharp, acidic, and minty aromas of herbs piled on the counter. Sage inhaled the fragrant scent and fresh herbal tea from a teapot brewing nearby.

"What do you think?" Will asked from behind her.

"I think these jars would be perfect for storing my ingredients," she said, pointing to the blue glass jars. "Do you mind having them and the ingredients delivered for me?"

Will nodded. "I think that's a great idea. Pick out your favorites, and I will have them sent over."

"Thank you, Will. I really appreciate it."

"Anytime, Sage. I'm always here to help." Will's eyes twinkled with affection.

Sage grabbed the jars she wanted and started a collection on the counter, making a mental note that she would need to ask about getting a set of shelves in her room to store all of this.

"Where were you having these delivered to?" Will asked, eyeing her curiously.

Sage was unsure if she should tell him the truth. But lying was not an option. After all, he only knew that she worked there. Not that it was home. She took a deep breath and exhaled before revealing her address to him.

Will's face changed as he dropped a jar of bright red mad honey onto the countertop with a loud thud. "You're working for the Charming Four?!"

"Yes," she said, keeping her tone nonchalant.

"They're dangerous, Sage," he said, his voice full of worry. "You should stay away from them."

"I can take care of myself, Will," she said with more confidence than she felt. "Besides, I need the money."

He shook his head solemnly. "If you need the extra money that badly, you can just work here. You know my father has offered before."

"I'm fine!" Sage snapped. "It's a good opportunity, and I need to do this on my own. I'm sorry, I need to go. I'm due at the library soon." She forced a smile and waved as she walked away. "Thank you, Will. You're the best."

The bell of the door dinged as she exited the apothecary. She felt guilty for snapping at him like that. She knew he was only looking out for her and appreciated the thought, but it also felt suffocating. She was an adult. She could do this.

**

Sage hurried back home, eager to see if the packages had arrived. She searched near the main entrance and in her room but found nothing. Disappointed and still somewhat frustrated, she made her way down the hallway when she heard a voice calling her name.

"Sage!" Asher shouted from the end of the hall. "I've been looking for you."

She stopped in her tracks, surprised that he was looking for her and curious why. He motioned for her to follow him to a room she hadn't seen before. She had yet to take the time to explore the house.

Asher gestured toward the shelves. "I bought you some supplies and set up a space for you to work. I know I sleep better if I don't have to sleep where I work."

Sage's eyes widened in amazement as she saw all the items neatly organized. Her blue jars were stacked on a row of shelves against the wall with plenty of space for more. Books sat on partially filled shelves, and a desk sat in front of a floor-to-ceiling stained glass window. A large table sat in the middle of the room with various tools on top.

"This is amazing!" Sage walked around the room.

"I'm sorry it took so long for me to get it set up; I ran into some complications."

"What kind of complications?" Sage asked curiously.

"It doesn't matter now," he said, smiling at her enthusiasm. "I can see how important your work is to you, and I want to ensure you have everything you need." He paused. "You know, I'm always around if you need anything else or just want someone to talk to."

A warm wave of emotion washed over Sage. She had felt so alone since her parents left, but Asher's thoughtfulness reminded her that she wasn't alone anymore. She smiled at him gratefully. "Thank you, Asher. I really appreciate this."

He nodded. "You're welcome. Now let's get to work. We've got a bit of time before dinner is ready. What are we making first?"

"We? You're offering to help?"

"I make no promises as to just how helpful my assistance will really be, but I'm willing to learn."

"Alright, let's think practically first. What do you have coming up? I know I'm not allowed to know details, but maybe a few hints to get a feel for what sort of things will be more helpful than others."

"There will be a ball at the castle soon. The crown prince's birthday. Any ideas for any special elixirs we could prepare for the occasion?" The glint in his eye told her that he was only partially joking. "We have no other quests or requests lined up right now. Once Prince Finn is fully healed, we will grab a new one and head out."

Sage laughed. "Well, I guess we should make an anti-love potion then, with how your group is with the ladies!"

"That does sound like something we may need one day!" Asher laughed.

"You think I'm kidding? Considering I'm working here because of a battle caused by two of your guild flirting, it wouldn't be a bad idea."

"You're actually serious. I didn't know there was such a thing."

"My father created several when he was young. My mother has a touch of a jealous streak, and it was her request early on in their marriage. Now, would something preventing other love potions from taking effect or something that would hinder romantic emotions from forming be the better option?"

Asher's jaw dropped, and no words left his mouth.

"I promise I will keep it mild. We don't want anyone outright hating the four of you. If we have enough time, we can do both."

A throat cleared, and Sage and Asher looked to find Prince Finn standing in the doorway. His stern eyes bore into her.

"Asher, we are ready for you," Prince Finn said.

Asher snapped out of it and offered Sage an apologetic smile as he left the room.

Prince Finn stayed an extra moment, not saying anything. His gaze still locked on her before flicking to take in the room. With a slight nod, he turned on his heel and left.

Sage took a breath and looked at the table in front of her. She shook her head and began arranging things so she could start working. It was going to be a long few nights.

***

Sage slowly stepped into Prince Finn's study, her hands clutching a cup of tea. Her heart raced with fear, yet her mind was set. She had come to fulfill a task, and though it terrified her, she steeled her soul and moved forward.

The prince sat behind a large oak desk dominating the room, surrounded by bookcases overflowing with ancient tomes.

Prince Finn looked up from his work as Sage stepped into the room. His eyes were deep and mysterious, a darkness that seemed to swallow her whole. Sage felt a chill run through her body as she realized who she was facing, and all her courage vanished.

Prince Finn nodded, his gaze still fixed on her. "And what is that?" He gestured towards the cup in her hands.

Sage looked down at the cup, her hands shaking slightly. She had prepared this in the hopes it might help prevent the Prince from turning into a gargoyle. She knew it was a long shot, but she had to start from somewhere.

"It's a tonic," she replied, her voice barely a whisper. "It's meant to help stop the transformation."

The Prince's eyes narrowed, as if he was attempting to read her mind. She could feel his gaze, like a heavy weight on her shoulders. She held her breath, hoping he would accept her offering.

Finally, after what felt like an eternity, the Prince spoke.

"Very well," he said. "Let us see what this potion can do."

He reached out and took the cup from her hand.
Before Sage could say anything, he had taken a sip.
His face contorted in revulsion as the foul taste hit
his tongue. He quickly put the cup down and let out
a loud and odorous burp.

Sage covered her nose with her hand, suppressing
a laugh as the smell hit her. She glanced at his hands
to see if his nails showed any change. There was
none.

It hadn't worked and now she had embarrassed
the Prince. She thought for a moment and then
offered an apology.

"I'm sorry, Your Highness," she said. "I-I hoped it
would have worked."

The Prince waved away her apology and smiled.
"It is of no consequence," he said. "I don't have high
hopes like the others. I've accepted my fate. I only
agreed because I know I would never hear the end
of it if I didn't."

Sage nodded, feeling a small sign of relief and a
twinge of pity towards the moody prince that sat in
front of her. She watched as the prince returned to
his work, and she quietly slipped from the room. As
she walked away, she allowed herself a small smile.
Perhaps her tonic hadn't worked, but something
about seeing him do something so ordinary made
him a tad less intimidating.

An Invitation for Trouble

"**W**hat are you doing here on your day off?"

Sage looked up from the pile of books on the table in the library cafe to find Piper tying an apron around her waist.

"A bit of research for a project I'm working on. I wasn't expecting you to be here today either."

Piper eyed the books. "I traded shifts to help my younger sister. Sage, why are you reading gargoyle romances and books about the magical effects of rocks?"

"I told you, research. It's for my part-time job. Even books of fiction can have hints of truth, so I pulled all of them that I could find." She put her napkin in the book and closed it, hoping that her friend hadn't seen just what section she was reading. Sage could tell that her face was bright red.

Piper winked. "Whatever you say," she replied with a grin. "Let me guess; you're reading them here so a certain gargoyle upstairs doesn't find out you are reading romance books about his species."

"He's not a species. According to *The History of Elemental Magical Mishaps*, gargoyles are fae. I'm studying how they are turned."

Piper glanced up at the second floor. "You're telling me that statue," she whispered, after leaning closer, "the one you've always been buddy-buddy with is actually a person? Is he cute? I'm assuming you've met him in his human form if you are researching something about his condition. Can I call it that?"

"Yes, I've met him. I guess he's sort of cute, and I have absolutely no idea what to call it yet."

"Alright, well, keep me updated. I shouldn't be late clocking in. By the way, did you get yours?"

"My what?"

Piper pulled a black envelope out of her pocket and placed it on the table. "Your invitation to the ball for the crowned prince. Everyone who works here will be invited. Can you imagine?! We get to go to a ball! Apparently, it's some charity thing, and the gifts will be used for the library."

A sinking feeling settled in Sage's gut. Hiding that she was connected to the Charming Four would be difficult if she went to the ball.

"Oh, yeah, of course," Sage said, trying to sound excited.

She opened the envelope, revealing a golden ticket with Piper's name written in beautiful calligraphy. A weight settled on her chest. She had to figure out how to go to the ball and keep her secret.

"I don't know. I've never been to one. I'm not really sure what I should do."

Piper laughed. "Just go and have fun! I'm sure you have the perfect dress in your closet somewhere."

"I don't have a closet, remember?"

"Oh, right," Piper said, her face falling. "That's right. Well, I can lend you something."

"You're sure?"

"Of course! I've got an idea that will be perfect."

Sage thought for a moment before nodding. "I'm willing to give it a try."

"It's settled then! You're going to the ball!" Piper tucked away the invitation and picked up the now-empty, blue-and-white tea cup from the table. "After I get off work, meet me at the main entrance. Let's find you a dress. Another white chocolate lavender latte?"

"You always know what to say to make me feel better."

***

Sage stretched her back as she walked out the library doors. She had stayed there all day and had around an hour before Piper got off. Sage left so she wasn't in the way while Piper cleaned up.

She couldn't help but feel overwhelmed by the thought of going to a royal ball. Sage was not accustomed to fancy events, and seeing elegant people adorned in beautiful clothing in a formal setting made her tremble with anxiety. She looked down at her worn dress and leather boots and sighed. Even if she found something suitable for a ball, it would not be nearly as dazzling as what everyone else would be wearing.

Lost in her thoughts, Sage didn't notice Asher until she bumped into him. Her eyes widened in alarm as she stumbled back, quickly apologizing for not paying attention. Asher looked at her in confusion before his face softened, and he smiled, gently touching her arm to steady her.

"Are you alright?" he asked kindly, still holding onto her arm.

The warmth of his fingers against her skin caused something inside her to stir. She found herself lost in his gaze, momentarily forgetting about the ball and the anxiety it caused. She was so captivated by him that she barely noticed when he released his grip on her arm.

"I'm fine," she said softly, her cheeks heating up. "What are you doing here?"

Asher seemed taken aback by the suddenness of her question. "I was taking care of something for my father. But what about you? What brings you here today?"

Sage felt embarrassed that she had forgotten her manners and shyly looked down at the ground. "Oh, uh, I was just waiting for a friend," she mumbled before looking back up at him with a small smile.

"You're an earth mage, right? And your family owns a gem mine?"

"Someone has been studying up on me. I am, and they do."

"When you have the time, I would love to ask you a few questions about rocks and magic," she said shyly.

Asher blinked in surprise before a wide grin spread across his face. "I have time now," he replied eagerly.

Sage's heart fluttered at his enthusiasm. He towered over her, partially blocking out the sun and when she looked up it was difficult to not melt a little into his deep brown eyes. She motioned for him to follow her as they walked away from the library to a nearby park. Sitting on opposite ends of the bench, she fidgeted as she figured out how to ask what she needed.

"You can ask me anything," he said, seeming to notice her fidgeting and giving her a reassuring smile. "If I'm uncomfortable answering, I'll let you know."

Sage hesitated before finally mustering the courage to ask her question. "Do you know what kind of stone gargoyles turn into?"

Asher's gaze on Sage, bore the weight of him deciding what to say. "Don't you have an actual gargoyle you can talk to about this?"

"I will ask him if I can't find the answers I need. Now that I live with you guys, it's not as easy to talk to Freddy. Besides, I thought you might have a unique look at the problem considering your personal experience."

"You should leave him a message. Write him a note and tuck it under his left heel near closing time. It's how we contact him when we need to. Usually with a time and place to meet up."

"I ... didn't think of that. Thank you."

"Of course. So about gargoyles. They're not exactly something I've studied, but I can tell you that my magic doesn't recognize what kind of stone they are. I've only encountered a couple, and each one felt different. I don't know if it's because they have different magic or were at different stages of the curse, but none felt like any stone I've encountered before."

Asher took a deep breath as he ran his hand through his chestnut hair. "I can tell you one thing, though. Their transformation is not something they can control. They still feel like themselves to me when they are stone. Even if I don't recognize their gargoyle form, my magic can still register who they are."

Sage thought about this for a moment before nodding. "That's actually really helpful. I'm glad I bumped into you."

"Likewise," Asher said, smiling.

Sage smiled in return, feeling a warm sensation in her chest.

"I should probably get going. I need to meet up with my friend soon."

"Oh, of course," Asher said, standing up from the bench. "It was great chatting with you. I'm looking forward to the next time we can do this again."

Sage smiled and nodded. "Me too." She watched as Asher turned and walked away.

Piper's smiling face approached her, interrupting her thoughts. "Sage! There you are! Are you ready to head out? I've got an idea for your dress!"

Sage grinned and took Piper's arm. She was grateful that she had bumped into Asher and they had been able to talk. With his advice, she had a better understanding of the gargoyle problem.

"Where are we off to?"

"Do you remember me telling you that I was late to help my sister?"

"Yeah..."

"She works at a clothing recycling company. People of all classes sell their clothing when they no longer need them and resold to others. Usually, it's worn-out clothing passed down from the middle class to the lower class, and the poorest sell their clothing for rags, but occasionally the wealthy bring in big batches of their clothing to sell as well. The richest wouldn't be caught dead wearing the same dress twice."

Sage felt a tiny flicker of hope. "So you think they may have a ball gown that I could buy? I can't afford to pay for a dress I'm only going to wear once."

"That's the genius of my idea. My sister is one of their seamstresses. She takes the dresses of the upper class and alters them before they resell them. I bet we can borrow a dress that she is altering."

"Piper, you just may be a genius."

The two girls made their way to a large brick building several blocks away. An unassuming sign hung over large wooden doors with Miracle Clothing Company written in large black letters.

As they entered the building, a woman wearing a bright smile greeted them. She wore a simple blue dress with her hair pulled back into a neat bun. "Welcome to Miracle Clothing Company! How can I help you?"

"Is Faith available? I'm her sister," Piper said.

"If you would follow me. She is working upstairs."

The woman led them up a broad flight of stairs, coming to a stop in front of a door with the word *Alterations* printed on it.

The woman opened the door and stepped aside, allowing them to enter. Faith was standing with her back to them, her brown hair cascading down to her shoulders. She was humming softly and seemed deeply engrossed in her work.

"Faith?" Piper said, stepping into the room.

Faith spun in surprise, her eyes widening when she saw Piper and Sage. "Piper! What are you two doing here?"

"Hoping you can help us." Piper pulled her invitation out and handed it to Faith. "We need dresses."

Faith smiled and gestured for them to follow her. She led them to a rack of dresses and began looking through them.

"Let's see what we have here," she said, eyes scanning the room.

Faith walked around pulling out different dresses, sifting through each one before setting it aside or returning it to its place on the rack. The selection was vast; there were long, flowing, lace gowns; sleek, satin, floor-length dresses; short chiffon numbers, and shimmering sequin sheaths.

After a few minutes of searching, Faith presented a glimmering ivory gown with a low V-neckline, a boned waist, a full skirt, and delicate beading along the bodice.

"This one is perfect. I can alter it to fit you perfectly. Add a few adjustments so it is fresh and new. Just be careful not to spill," Faith said with a smile.

Sage couldn't believe her luck. She carefully took the gown, holding it out, and taking a twirl.

"Thank you so much! This will be perfect," Sage said, her excitement growing with each passing second before handing the dress back to Faith.

Faith smiled and winked at her sister. "Now, what should you wear?"

***

Sage stood in her workroom. The setting sun reflected a kaleidoscope of colors on the floor through the stained-glass windows.

Everything was almost ready. The ball was in a few hours, with both anti-love potions prepared.

A blue bottle with a glass roller on top held an antidote to prevent people from developing romantic feelings. This would need to be rolled onto each man's pulse points before they left to ensure they didn't wear too much. In contrast, she had prepared individual bottles with a counteragent to any potential love potions.

The last thing Sage needed was for the Charming Four to go to a royal ball and find that everyone hated them, thanks to her work.

She double-checked her work, making sure the dosage was perfect. She focused on the task at hand, blocking out the doubts in her mind. The Charming Four had been nothing but friendly to her, well, most of them, since she started working for them, and she wanted to make sure her work was as perfect as possible.

Picking up the bottles, Sage left the room.

As she stepped into the hallway, Sage was startled by another person who had also been walking by. Her grip on one of the bottles loosened in a moment of panic, causing it to slip out of her hands and crash to the floor. Shards of glass flew everywhere as the contents spilled out and splattered on the other person's front in an iridescent red liquid.

To Sage's horror, it was Prince Finn.

He stared at her with such intensity that she thought he would yell at her. But instead, he bent down and carefully collected the pieces of glass, not saying a word.

Sage dropped to her knees and placed the bottles on the ground. "Stop. You need to remove any wet clothing this instant," she said.

"Excuse me?"

"I can clean this up. Do not let that touch your skin. That was one of the anti-love potions. If too much absorbs into your skin, fights will break out for reasons other than lust."

The prince looked at her, unmoving.

Sage waved her hand at him expectantly before he rolled his eyes and stood to strip off his shirt.

She held out her hand to take it. "I can clean it for you. Plus, it will be safer for me to pick these shards up with your shirt than my bare hands. The last thing I need is to get too much on my skin and have the four of you decide I'm an enemy. I'm pretty sure I wouldn't survive that outcome."

Sage's heart pounded as the prince reluctantly handed her his shirt and stepped away from the mess. His muscular chest was pale in the hallway's light. Sage's eyes kept making their way to the prince, which she quickly remedied, feeling embarrassed and a little ashamed of herself.

"Do you have more in reserve now that it's covering my clothing, or are we out of luck for the night?"

"I have a small amount that didn't fit in the bottle. You probably shouldn't apply any tonight, though. I don't know how much has gotten on you."

Prince Finn didn't reply, which Sage took as her cue to finish cleaning the mess.

She quickly scooped up all the pieces she could see, placing them inside the prince's shirt and tying it so that they were safely contained before cleaning up whatever oil had spilled on the floor. Careful not to let it get on her.

When she finished, she carefully held up the bottles again, looking between them and then back at Prince Finn. Careful to avoid staring at his bare chest. He stared back at her with a quizzical expression as if he was waiting for something else from her.

Sage swallowed hard. "There's one for each of you. Can you deliver these after you change? Make sure you drink all of it before going to the ball."

Prince Finn nodded and took the remaining three bottles. "We will. Thank you for your help," he said before turning away to get changed.

Sage felt a mixture of emotions. On the one hand, she was relieved that her clumsiness hadn't ruined the night and could now focus on getting ready for the ball, but on the other, she was embarrassed and ashamed that she had been clumsy enough to cause this mess in the first place.

But she had done her job, and hopefully, no one would ever find out what had happened there tonight.

The Ball

S age made her way to her room, feeling the day's fatigue wash over her. How would she make it through tonight when she was already this exhausted?

She had just reached her room when she saw a large black box outside her door. She swung the door open and carried it into her room, placing it on her bed.

Her heart pounded as she slowly untied the ribbon and opened the top. Inside was a beautiful dress and a note.

Sage,
I didn't have enough time to change up the dress completely, but I did a few minor alterations and sent over some accessories to complete the look. Have fun, and remember to return this tomorrow!
-Faith

The sparkling stones on top remained unchanged, but Sage gasped in surprise at how stunning it was once she removed the dress from the box. It was much more beautiful than anything she had ever seen before.

The bottom of the ivory dress had been covered in delicate but sharp swirls made from gold lace ap-pliques climbing up the dress as if it were frost. The dress felt entirely transformed.

She couldn't believe it was hers, even if just for one night, and held it against herself before twirling in delight.

She had to admit that she was starting to look forward to tonight. The last thing she wanted was to miss the ball because of her clumsiness.

Sage quickly changed out of her regular clothing and into her new ball gown, admiring herself in the mirror as she twirled in delight. In the reflection something caught her eye. Still inside the black box was a small blue one.

Sage opened it to find the most beautiful jewelry she had ever seen. It wasn't a necklace, bracelet, or even earrings. No, this was so much more than that.

Opening the clasp, Sage slipped it on and fastened it. It was stunning. Five strings of blue and clear gems set in gold stretched across her collarbone, connecting her shoulders in a swoop.

Spinning around to look at the back, she was surprised to find a collection of long strands of varied stones layered over her back. The top three were gathered with what Sage assumed was a pin with a large, oval, dark-blue stone surrounded by small clear ones.

The closer Sage looked at the elaborate piece, the more she realized that this was probably a collection created from necklaces and bracelets.

Sage thought what a clever woman Faith was. She not only created something unique and beautiful but something that she could easily take apart after tonight and turn into anything else she desired.

Sage was tempted to take it off and leave it at home. The value of the jewelry had to be more than Sage would earn over her lifetime, but another look in the mirror and she changed her mind. It made this outfit something special.

Sage allowed herself a moment more to admire the piece of jewelry that was now adorning her body. Somehow it felt as if her brown hair set off the blue around her neck and shoulders in a way that surely only she would notice. She twisted her long hair back into a low bun and allowed a few pieces of hair to fall around her face.

She put on some light blush and a touch of color on her lips, just enough to make her look radiant and beautiful for the night ahead.

As Sage stood back up and took a final look in the mirror, she felt ready for anything the ball would throw at her.

***

Sage emerged from the castle's hallway and stepped into the grand ballroom.

Piper had picked her up in a rented carriage at Faith's insistence. It made sense to Sage. She couldn't imagine how she would have made it to the castle without her dress' hem becoming filthy from the muddy streets.

From the moment she had arrived, Sage was immediately awestruck by the ballroom's grandeur—it was unlike anything she had ever seen. A stunning mix of marble and gold, with intricate patterns, dec-orated every wall.

Large crystal chandeliers hung from the ceiling, their light reflecting off the marble floor in a mesmerizing fashion. Along one side of the room stood an elegant white grand piano, and on the opposite were two large staircases leading up to a balcony that overlooked the entire room.

Fine linens, silverware, and ornate centerpieces filled with colorful fresh flowers, each more beautiful than the last, adorned the long tables along a third wall. Everywhere Sage looked, there seemed to be something new to admire; whether it was an exquisite set of chairs or a sculpture made entirely out of flowers, it seemed as if the designer had left no details overlooked.

"Are you ready?" Piper asked.

Their turn to be announced was coming up. Only two people stood in line in front of them.

Sage fidgeted with the gold on her skirt. "Not in the slightest. You?"

"I'm so nervous I think I may get sick," Piper laughed, holding her hand to the corset of her burgundy dress. Floral embroidery covered most of the dress in a variety of colors. The live flowers woven into her hair and delicate jewelry made her best friend appear as if she were a fairy.

"Come on," Sage said, lightly taking her arm. "We can do this. We aren't anyone that people will notice, and as soon as we get in, we can just enjoy the good food and people-watch!"

"I would love to dance too."

Sage laughed. "You can dance for both of us. It's best if I stay off the dance floor."

Together they walked forward, their names announced with a flourish, and descended the stairs. Sage could feel countless eyes watching her every move. Though her heart was beating faster than ever, Sage managed to keep her composure.

As soon as they reached the bottom of the steps, the next group was called, and Piper and Sage let out a unanimous sigh of relief.

The night was finally theirs to enjoy.

They found a spot to hide in the corner, where they could still see the grand entrance and the dances but remained hidden.

Piper started to relax as she observed the other guests. She pointed out the Charming Four on the other side of the ballroom.

They were in deep conversation with a group of men and women. The group laughed. Sage noted that the women placed their hands delicately on the men's arms as they did so, but not on the Charming Four.

She smiled to herself. It appeared her anti-love potions were working.

As the evening progressed, the two watched the people meandering around, and Sage couldn't help but feel forlorn for not being able to participate in the festivities. Although the ball was grand and beautiful, Sage felt a distinct longing as the other guests danced and laughed.

It didn't take long for a few of the men to take notice of Piper. A tall, broad-shouldered man with light brown hair and sapphire eyes approached her.

"Would you care to dance?" he asked, a romantic look in his eyes.

Piper smiled and gave him a single nod before taking his hand, and they disappeared into the crowd, swept away by music and laughter.

Suddenly feeling alone and uncomfortable, Sage wandered over to the food table and grabbed a small plate.

The table held all sorts of beautiful delicacies, small pastries filled with custard, chocolate, and cream. There were fruits of every kind: bananas, oranges, apples, cherries, and pears. Many of these fruits she had never seen before and could only imagine how they tasted.

Sage reached for a pastry first, picking it up by its leaf-like plate. It was golden, with a sticky syrup, causing it to stick to the plate. The pastry was soft and warm, with a savory sweetness that melted in her mouth.

She let out a small moan of happiness as a dark-haired man approached her.

"I'm glad to see that someone is enjoying the food. I hate how no one eats at these events." His voice was soft yet confident. "Such a waste. To be fair, most have a healthy avoidance of fae food. You never know what it will do to you."

Sage could feel her cheeks heat up. "I'm sorry. I didn't mean to be so ... enthusiastic."

The man smiled and shook his head. "No, don't be sorry. It's nice to see someone who can appreciate something so small."

He reached out his hand. "My name's Owen."

Sage took his hand and nodded. "Sage."

"It's a pleasure to meet you. Welcome to my birthday party."

Sage's stomach dropped. This wasn't just anyone. This was the crown prince. Prince Finn's brother.

"Oh, I didn't realize..." She could feel her cheeks turning red.

"It's quite alright. I'm sure many people here don't know who I am. They may know my name but not my face." He smiled, seemingly amused by her confusion.

Sage couldn't help but smile back. "Thank you, Your Highness," she said, curtsying.

Prince Owen just laughed. "No need to be so formal. We can be friends, right?"

Sage laughed. "Yes, of course. If that's what you wish."

He offered her his arm. "Would you care to dance then?"

"Only if you promise not to throw me in the dungeon for stepping on your toes."

"That bad?"

"You have been warned. I'm truly terrible at dancing." She took his arm and followed Prince Owen onto the dance floor.

"One of your few flaws, I'm sure."

Sage snorted before she noticed his face held no humor. "Oh, you were serious."

The arch of his brow made her melt a little. "I don't give out compliments unless I feel they are deserved."

"Perhaps you should know someone longer than a minute before offering such compliments if you want to keep that reputation."

The twinkle in his eye told her he was enjoying the banter as much as she was. Why he had picked her out of the crowd to dance with was beyond her, but she had to admit that Prince Owen was much easier to please than his brother.

The music began to play, and Sage tried her best to keep up with the steps. She stumbled a few times, but Prince Owen's hand caught her each time and gently guided her back into the dance.

"You're doing amazingly," he said with a smile.

Sage's face heated up again. She was so embarrassed. She had expected him to be disappointed, but he was complimenting her instead.

"Thank you."

"So," he said in a low voice as they moved around the floor. "What do you do?"

"I'm a librarian at your family's library. It's how I got the invitation for tonight."

Prince Owen nodded. "I see. That must be quite interesting."

"It can be," Sage said, her cheeks still feeling warm. "I love books and learning the secrets between their pages."

"I imagine that keeps you busy."

"It does. I also work part-time as an apothecary, but..." Sage realized what she was saying and who she was saying it to. He gave her a curious look. "I'm still learning and figuring some stuff out with that, though," she rambled before he could ask anything else.

Prince Owen smiled. "Well, I'm sure you'll get there eventually. I know it can take time to really get the hang of things."

The music came to an end and she stepped back and bowed.

"Thank you, Your Highness," she said quietly.

"It was my pleasure."

Sage wanted to find Piper but bumped into something behind her.

"Finn, it's good of you to come," Prince Owen said.

"I could never miss my brother's birthday, even if I wanted to."

Sage glanced between the two brothers. It was clear they were related. Both had the same dark hair, tall stature, and classic good looks, but something in their eyes made them seem so different. While Prince Owen had an easy smile and a playful glint in his eye, Prince Finn's gaze was more intense and guarded.

Prince Owen clapped his brother on the shoulder. "It's good to see you," he said warmly.

"You too," Prince Finn replied curtly.

The two brothers exchanged a few more words before Prince Owen excused himself to greet other guests. Sage watched him walk away before looking to Prince Finn with a polite smile.

The two stood silent before Sage gave a slight bow.

"Have a good evening, Your Highness," she whispered, then turned to leave. She made her way over to a set of doors and slipped onto the balcony. Why did she always feel as if she were in trouble with Prince Finn? He seemed so cold and distant whenever they crossed paths, while his brother was warm and inviting.

Sage sighed as she leaned against the railing, taking in the city's stunning night view. People were dancing and celebrating a few feet away, but something about it all seemed so far away from where she stood now.

A shadow appeared behind her, blocking the ballroom's light. She spun and found herself face-to-face with Prince Finn. He didn't smile at her, but his gaze held an unforeseen gentleness.

"What are you doing out here?" he asked, his voice low and quiet.

Sage swallowed nervously. "I-I just wanted some ... some fresh air," she stammered.

Prince Finn nodded and stepped closer, gazing into her eyes as if searching for something deep within her soul.

"You seem troubled," he said, his voice barely more than a whisper in the night air.

The comment surprised Sage; she wasn't sure how to respond, so she shook her head.

Prince Finn stepped closer and reached up to brush a stray hair from her face with a gentle touch of his fingertips. He looked down at her. Their eyes locked for just a few seconds and it felt like no one else existed but Prince Finn and Sage before she pulled away.

"You need to be careful," Prince Finn said.

"Of what?" Sage asked, her voice barely audible.

Prince Finn chewed his lip as if he were at war with himself. "Of my brother. He isn't what he seems."

"So says the grump who doesn't want anything to do with me. Why do you care?"

"I don't. I just don't like seeing anyone in my care get hurt."

"I'm in your care?"

"You are one of my staff, are you not?"

Sage put some space between them and her back hit the railing.

"If I am only part of your staff, I believe you have no say in who I spend my free time with. But tell me. Why do I need to avoid your brother?"

Prince Finn ran his hand through his hair and let out a huff. "You don't know what he is capable of, what he has done, what he enjoys doing. He only cares for power and how he can get more while securing what he already has." Prince Finn paused. "My brother is cunning and will do anything to get what he wants. He does not care about anyone else's feelings or well-being. He will use you and discard you just as quickly."

Sage took a deep breath and exhaled slowly. "So you are warning me to watch out for him because he may treat me like you do?"

Prince Finn stared at her. "Excuse me? When have I ever used you?"

Her anger boiled over, and Sage stormed closer to Prince Finn. "You. Attacked. Me. In. The. Library," she spat, her finger pushing into his chest with each point.

"I never touched you. It was a war of words where I was educating you, and to be fair, the first time I saw you in the library, you acted as if you were a crazed woman."

"You trapped me in your house!" she growled as she poked again. "I wouldn't put it past you to have orchestrated the entire thing for me to live there now out of spite for me turning you down the first time."

"Sage, I didn't know you even knew how to heal anyone until that battle against the dark guild."

"I'm sure you didn't," Sage mumbled as she pushed him again. "Do you know that every single time we interact, I leave feeling like I'm worthless? Like I am inferior and can't do anything right? I can't think of a single interaction we've had so far where I haven't left feeling that way!"

Prince Finn leaned in until his lips were next to her ear. "Even when you asked me to strip in the hallway earlier today?"

Sage shoved him away and backed against the railing again.

"Will you stop doing that!" Prince Finn yelled. "If you don't, I will toss you off this balcony myself."

Sage glanced behind her and looked back at him with a sly smile.

"What were you doing?" he asked.

"Looking to see how far of a drop it is."

"Don't you dare—" He didn't have a chance to finish what he was saying before Sage hopped up on the railing, threw her legs over the edge, and dropped.

Sage landed on soft grass, rolled a few times, and looked up to see Prince Finn hovering at the balcony's edge, looking down at her in shock. She winked at him and waved before standing up and walking off.

Her heart was pounding, and her mind was racing with what had just happened. She had done something way beyond her usual boundary, and it felt both exhilarating and terrifying.

Shaking her head, she pushed the thoughts away and continued walking through the palace gardens. She was amazed at how vast and detailed everything was. Topiaries were shaped into various animals, trees covered with bright flowers in full bloom, and lit lanterns glowing along the paths. The air was sweet with the smell of jasmine, honeysuckle, and the musk of several different breeds of roses.

Every couple of steps Sage took brought her closer to what she assumed was the palace ground's main gate. But before reaching it, Sage heard voices behind a large bush and stopped in her tracks.

Peeking around it, Sage saw Asher standing with a woman with her arm wrapped around his waist as though they were old acquaintances. The woman had curly dark hair cascading down her back, and deep brown eyes sparkled as she looked up at Asher with admiration.

He seemed to be enjoying the attention as he regarded her warmly.

Sage felt an odd pang of something inside her chest.

She wasn't sure if it was jealousy or something else, but before she could overthink it, the two started walking away, and Sage quickly ducked back behind the bush.

Once they were out of sight, she stood and brushed the dirt off her dress. She almost wished she had asked Asher how to reach the exit but didn't want to get in the way of whatever she had just witnessed. Especially with the reaction she had just experienced.

Taking deep breaths to calm herself down, Sage continued on her path toward the exit. With every step she took, she got closer and closer, but it seemed like no matter how far she walked, she couldn't find it.

She finally reached a part of the garden with a small pond and decided to take a break. Sitting on a nearby bench, she watched the fish swim around in pairs, darting in and out of the lilies scattered among the pond's surface.

Sage sighed in relief as her heart rate started to slow. She had almost given up hope before coming across this peaceful spot.

A voice broke the silence of the peaceful garden. It was Prince Owen, and he seemed to be in a heated argument with someone else. Sage was curious about who it was, so she crept closer against her better judgment. Sage couldn't hear what they were saying clearly, but from the sound of their voices, it wasn't anything pleasant.

Before Sage could reach them, someone grabbed her arm and pulled her back into the bushes. Her head whipped around to see who it was. To her surprise, it was Prince Finn beside her.

"What are you doing here?" she whispered.

"Shhh," he hissed before looking back to ensure no one had seen them.

Sage's heart rate increased as Prince Finn's face filled with intense emotions; anger, worry, and determination all rolled into one expression that sent a chill down her spine. He held his finger to his lips, motioning for her to stay quiet.

Sage nodded, not daring to make a sound. She was pressed against his chest, seated on his legs in the small space. She could feel his heart racing. She hoped he couldn't feel hers.

"I haven't found her," the unknown man's voice carried on the wind.

"She's basically their pet at this point. Find my brother and his friends, and you should find her. Bring her to my room without being seen," Prince Owen replied.

Sage felt her stomach drop as the realization dawned on her. They had to be talking about her.

"We need to go before they see us," Prince Finn whispered into her ear.

Sage couldn't do anything but nod and follow him out of the bushes.

"Let's get you out of here," he said, taking her hand once they were on the path.

She attempted to free her hand from his, but Prince Finn didn't let go. Shooting him a dirty look, she allowed him to lead her around the palace grounds until they eventually came to the exit.

The palace gate towered in front of them.

"Promise me," he said, his voice low and steady. "Promise me you will be careful around Prince Owen. I don't know what he wants, but it can't be good."

Sage looked up at him and nodded. "I promise."

Prince Finn offered a small smile and let go of her hand. He called a carriage over, helped her into it, and followed her inside.

"Don't you need to go back to the ball?" Sage asked.

"No," he replied simply. Confused, she fixed her skirts as he instructed the driver to take them home. "I've made my appearance."

Prince Finn watched out the window as the city passed them by. "Things are happening in this kingdom that people don't like to talk about. People who find themselves to be above others and see nothing wrong with using others as if they were objects. Secrets from the past that, if they came to light, would change everything."

Sage was taken aback by his candor. "Is your mission part of that?"

He sat back and was silent again, looking at the passing scenery with a somber expression.

She decided not to press him any further. Instead, she took the rest of the silent ride home to contemplate the prince.

Perhaps he wasn't as bad as she first thought.

The Crown Prince's Request

S he opened the door of her apothecary and stepped inside, feeling safe and surrounded by familiar things. She soon settled into work, putting on an apron and tying her hair back.

It had been a long day at the library, and she was excited to get some time to herself.

If he received the note she had left according to Asher's instructions, Freddy should be coming by after dark so she could talk to him about his condition. She didn't know if the Charming Four would be gone at the time, but Sage had no issues being alone with him. After all, they had lived together for a short time.

So she just needed to keep busy until he got there.

The room was warm and comforting, filled with the scent of herbs and flowers. Sage smiled as she began her work, sorting through her supplies, pouring ingredients into large ceramic vats, and stirring them until they were the right consistency.

Sage worked for hours on end, lost in the creation of her potions, salves, and tinctures. Her mind was free from the worries of the kingdom. Instead, it ran wild with possibilities, possibilities that could exist within a simple life like hers.

She had been experimenting with new recipes recently, and tonight she wanted to try something different. She decided to create a calming tonic to help lessen stress or tension in those who consumed it. Maybe even try it herself and get caught up on some sleep. She collected several herbs, such as chamomile, lavender, and lemon balm, before crushing them up into a paste.

Once she finished that, she added tiny droplets of frankincense and eucalyptus oils.

Sage worked diligently, turning her mind away from thoughts of the Charming Four. She moved from one herb to the next, mixing ingredients and creating different concoctions. As the day drew to a close, contentment filled her—until she heard a faint knock on the front door. The few servants in the house had gone to bed already, but her work-room was only down the hall from the main entrance making it easy to hear. She hurried to answer it, the house silent.

When she opened the door, Sage was surprised to find Prince Owen standing at the entrance alone. His gaze was intense as if he had been waiting for *her* to answer. Sage stood frozen, unable to move or speak. Prince Finn's warning fresh in her mind, she took a step back and silently cursed herself for not being more careful.

She steadied herself. "Your Highness ... what can I do for you?"

Prince Owen smiled. "I remembered you were quite talented in making potions, and I have need of something ... special."

"I wouldn't necessarily say *quite* talented. If I remember correctly, I said that I am still learning."

Prince Owen stepped forward, his presence dominating the atmosphere. "I'm sure you can help us, right, Sage?"

His words lingered in the air, making Sage feel she had no choice.

She nodded slowly. "Yes, of course."

He gave her a large grin, seemingly satisfied with her answer.

Holding the door open, she welcomed him inside and led him to a sitting room. She felt uneasy being alone in the house with him.

Sage hoped Freddy would show up soon.

Prince Owen sat near the fire on one of the wing-back chairs. She took the one opposite and waited for Prince Owen to speak first.

"I need a calming tonic to help people relax and feel at peace. Can you create something like that?"

Sage remembered the concoction she had been working on earlier.

"Yes, I believe so. Anyone with a basic understanding of tinctures and potions could. Why do you need me?"

Prince Owen paused before reaching into his pocket and pulling out a large green scale.

Sage instantly recognized it as a dragon scale. She had heard stories of people using dragon scales to craft powerful potions but had never seen one in person. After all, dragons had been wiped out long ago, so any item left by a dragon that still existed was hard to find.

"Do you think you could include this in it to help amplify the effects?" the prince asked.

Sage was leery. If that was what she thought it was, it would turn her relaxing potion into a deadly one. She looked at the scale with trepidation, unsure of the prince's true purpose or safety implications. Did she have a choice, though? No one could say no to the crown prince.

"I can do that," she said, careful to disguise her uncertainty. "When do you need it by?"

"Tonight would be best."

Sage nodded, swallowing the lump in her throat, then rose from her chair, taking the scale from his hand.

"Sage." His voice stopped her.

She turned, motionless, and looked at him. His gaze seemed to penetrate her as if he could sense her fear.

"Thank you for your help."

"Of course. Would you like some tea with honey while I work? I should have offered earlier."

"That would be wonderful. Thank you."

Sage forced a smile and excused herself as she returned to her workroom. She couldn't help but feel like she was walking a dangerous path. What was Prince Owen up to? No doubt he came expecting her to be inexperienced and not know what that scale was. She couldn't help him create something this dangerous.

Once in her workspace, Sage set the dragon scale on the table and began preparing tea.

She pulled out a small copper kettle of water, setting it to warm over the fire while she collected a wooden tray laden with cups painted with delicate red roses. After heating the water, she turned to face her shelves, deciding what to put in the tea. Her eyes drifted over colorful herbs, jars of honey and sugar, and sprigs of different flowers and spices.

Her eyes darted back to the honey and an idea formed. One that could possibly get her killed if anyone found out, but if it worked, it would buy her time. The time that she needed to figure out what to do.

She reached up and carefully pulled down the bottle of mad honey, a small bowl, and a honey wand. She placed the bowl on the tray, slowly poured the bright red sweetener into it, and stuck the wand inside. The teapot whistled and she removed it from the heat, placing it on the tray with the cup and bowl of honey.

Gathering her ingredients, Sage took all of them to the sitting room.

Her gaze went to Prince Owen from across the room, who seemed mesmerized by the fire dancing before him.

"You're back."

Her hands shaking slightly, she walked over and placed the tray on a table beside the prince. She served the tea and put honey in it, not daring to look into his eyes as she stirred the mixture.

"Thank you," Prince Owen said after taking a sip.

Sage nodded slightly, her heart racing.

Prince Owen continued to sip the tea, seemingly satisfied with the taste. He looked at her with a smile.

"It's perfect. Thank you, Sage."

Sage couldn't help but worry about the consequences of having given him the honey. It wasn't just any honey. Mad honey only was available from one area of the kingdom, and it deserved its name. A small amount made a grown man hallucinate. Slightly more than that left him dead.

"I should get to work," Sage said with a slight bow as she picked up the tray and returned to her workspace.

She was relieved to be away from Prince Owen's intense gaze and the worry that lingered in the air. Once in the safety of her workspace, she began on the calming tonic. Listening intently for sounds from the sitting room or the door announcing Freddy's arrival.

Working quickly, she mixed the herbs and essential oils, adding the dragon scale and a few drops of safe-to-eat honey to make it more palatable. While she never thought it helped, her father swore by it. When done, she added the concoction to a vial and stoppered it securely. Her stomach churned with unease, not knowing what would happen when someone consumed it.

Just as she was putting the vial away, Sage heard a knock at the door. Her heart leaped with joy—it must be Freddy. She hurried to answer it and was relieved and joyful to see Freddy. His eyes twinkled jovially as he smiled at her.

"Freddy!" She hugged him tightly. "I'm so glad you're here."

Freddy laughed, taking a step back. "I'm used to women being excited to see me," he said, smiling, "but not this excited."

Sage smiled, feeling embarrassed. She gestured for him to come in.

"There's something I need your help with," she said, leading him into the sitting room.

"What is it?" Freddy asked curiously.

Sage was about to answer when they entered the room to find Prince Owen arguing with the curtain. The curtains swayed in response.

Prince Owen, his face livid, shouted something at the curtain, defending his good name. Sage took an involuntary step back in surprise, her eyes wide and incredulous.

Freddy studied the interaction between Prince Owen and the curtain.

"What's going on here," he asked as he motioned to the prince.

Prince Owen turned to them, his face still contorted in rage, before quickly composing himself into a more regal expression. He cleared his throat.

"I'm sorry you had to witness that," he said with a hint of embarrassment. "My brother always tends to think the worst of me." He gestured toward the curtain, which seemed to shimmer ever so slightly.

"If you will excuse us for a moment, Prince Owen. Let me get you something to eat with your tea," Sage o ered.

Prince Owen nodded absently, and Sage jerked her head for Freddy to follow her. After she closed the door behind them, she led Freddy to her workroom and held up the vial.

"How much do you know about potions?" she asked.

"Quite a bit. Why?" Freddy took in her workspace until his eyes snagged on the bottle that Sage held. "What's that?"

"It's why the prince is here. He asked me to make a calming potion with dragon scale."

Freddy's eyes shot from the bottle to her eyes in surprise. "And you did it?"

"Have you ever had anything good come from telling anyone of the royal family no?"

"You have a point. We can fix this. First, tell me what's wrong with the crown prince. Did he show up here like that?"

Sage pointed at the bottle of mad honey still on the table behind her.

"I gave him a tiny amount of that. Not enough to cause any harm."

Freddy's brow rose. "That would explain his behavior. You know you can lose your head for pulling this stunt."

"I didn't know what else to do!"

"I know. I'm not blaming you."

She set the bottle on the table and crossed her arms while Freddy shook his head.

"Alright, maybe I blame you a little bit," he said, pacing around the table. "This is what we will do. You will add toadwart to that potion Prince Owen asked you to make. It will still make people appear dead without actually killing them ... generally. I assume you have some."

Walking to the shelves, she pulled down the bottle with toadwart. "It appears so."

"Good. I will have a few drinks with the crowned prince, so when he leaves here, he will chalk all of this up to the alcohol, and hopefully, no suspicion will fall onto you. When you finish up, join us, and we will get him out of here as quickly as possible."

Sage nodded. "I can do that. There's no alcohol in the sitting room. Where are you going to grab some?"

Freddy winked and smiled. " I know where the boys keep the good stuff."

Sage nodded and set to work, grateful for Freddy's help in this precarious situation. She added the toadwart to the bottle, and with a quick wipe to clean any spilled drops, she headed to the sitting room to deliver it.

As she entered, she approached the two men sitting on either side of the fireplace and handed it to Prince Owen.

"This is it," she said, not quite meeting his eyes.

He nodded and accepted the vial, tucking it away into his pocket.

"Thank you for your help, Sage. I am sure this will be of great use. I'll be sure to remember your assistance."

"You really don't have to," Sage muttered under her breath through a small forced smile.

He stood and offered a tiny wave goodbye to Freddy and her before taking his cloak and heading to the door. Sage followed and locked it as soon as it closed, relief hitting her now that it was finally over. She was sure to receive some kind of reprimand for her actions, but she seemed to have gotten away with it right now.

Freddy sat in the chair, a glass of ruby-red liquid in his hand. "That was close," he said with a smile before taking a sip.

Sage nodded and sat in the chair opposite him.

"Did he say anything else?" she asked.

"No," Freddy said, shaking his head. "He was in a hurry. I think he was worried about being discovered. He didn't say much. Mostly mumbled nonsense to himself."

Sage nodded, relieved.

"Well," Freddy said, leaning back in his chair beside the fire, "unless you have suddenly developed the ability to see into the future, I'm assuming that's not why you invited me over."

Sage smiled and shook her head.

"No, it's not. I wanted to thank you for everything and ask you a few questions about the gargoyle curse."

"Of course," he said. "You know I'm always here for you, Sage. We're friends, after all. Ask away. What do you want to know?"

Sage took a deep breath.

"Do you know what gargoyles turn into?" That question had been burning in her mind for so long. "I mean, what actual stone do you become when you transition into a gargoyle?"

Freddy shook his head, his expression solemn.

"No," he said slowly. "When a fae transitions into a gargoyle, they look and feel like stone." He paused, rubbing his chin. "There are rumors that this transformation is not only physical but metaphysical as well—the essence of your being becomes intertwined with the stone, and thus it is unique and able to protect you from harm."

Sage stared at him. "That's incredible."

Freddy smirked. "Did you just call me incredible?"

Sage laughed. "It's not how I meant it but you're welcome to interpret it that way. I would never accept someone as my friend if they were anything less," she teased.

Freddy chuckled as he took another sip from his glass. They turned toward the fire, their conversation coming to a comfortable pause. The flames crackled and popped, and Sage stared into the embers, feeling the warmth on her face.

"Does it hurt?" Sage asked, her gaze still on the fire.

Freddy shook his head. "No, not at all. It's a peaceful transition, and when it's complete, you feel as if you've just woken from the most restful slumber imaginable. The beginning stages before your first shift are uncomfortable. Your body becomes stiff during the day, and a numbness creeps in."

Sage's thoughts drifted to Prince Finn. Was he having those sorts of issues already?

"Do you think the prince ... ?"

"Yes?" Freddy's voice brought her back to the present.

"Never mind."

"No, he won't be shifting for a few more years yet. He's far too early in the stages. You have plenty of time to devise a way to fix both of us before that happens. I've basically quit using my magic, so it's not getting worse for me."

"You mean other than to help others check out the books in the library?"

"True, other than that."

"Why the 'Twinkle, Twinkle, Little Dragon' song to check out books? Is it an actual spell?"

Freddy laughed. "Not in the slightest. It started out as a joke, and I decided to keep it. They don't have to say anything to check out a book. Only place their card and book in my stone hands."

"You didn't! Is that why Prince Finn didn't check out the book?"

"Not even he knows. He just didn't want to sing the song."

Sage poured herself a glass as she chuckled. "That sounds like him."

Sage couldn't help but wonder if Freddy was lonely. Thoughts of who he may have left behind because of the curse and giving him an unusually long life floated through her mind. She would never pry and ask him directly, but she hoped he had found some peace with what cards fate had given him.

Honeybee

S age ambled through the vast aisles of the royal library, her fingers trailing along the spines of leather-bound books. An idea struck her after her incident with the crown prince last night, but she needed to research before she dared to start testing her theory. She had been hunting for a particular tome all day, one that held the secrets of the magical medicinal uses of honey.

She sighed, feeling the weight of her burden. She felt that she was close to figuring out a treatment for the gargoyle curse, and she refused to give up now.

"Sage, is that you?" a voice called behind her.

Sage spun to see Piper standing at the end of the row of books, a massive smile on her face. She was holding Sage's favorite mug filled with steamy liquid.

"What have you got there?" Sage asked, motioning to the mug.

"You seemed off today, so I brought you your favorite drink," Piper said, her eyes twinkling. "It's a white chocolate lavender latte, just how you like it."

Her heart fluttered. No one knew her better than Piper, and she was always thoughtful.

"Thank you," Sage said, taking the mug from her. "This will definitely help me get through this search, at least for a little bit."

"I thought it might," Piper said, still smiling. "Now, tell me what you're looking for. I know you wouldn't be here for hours if it weren't important."

Sage took a sip of the latte, savoring the sweet taste, before telling Piper about her encounter with the crowned prince and her quest for the book.

"That sounds dangerous, Sage. If the crown prince ever figures out what you did to him, you could be in serious trouble. Not to mention when the potion you gave him doesn't do what you told him it would do. What are you going to do then?"

Sage sighed heavily and looked at her friend. "I know it's dangerous, and I'm not sure what I'm going to do if he figures it out. But I'm hoping that if I can find this book and learn more about the magical medicinal uses of honey, I can come up with something to at least slow down Freddy and Prince Finn's curse. Take care of one problem at a time. Deal with whatever happens with Prince Owen when it happens."

Piper nodded slowly and put a hand on Sage's shoulder. "I understand. If there's anyone who can figure this out, it's you. Do you need any help? I know the Charming Four have a lot of magical knowledge. They are also probably your best bet for protection from Prince Finn's brother."

Sage shook her head. "No, I think I need to do this alone. But thank you for the offer. I should probably get back to looking for that book. It's incredible how some of the older sections of the library are completely in disarray. I can't find anything. You can really tell which sections Freddy has less interest in."

"And you?"

"Alright, you've got me there."

"If anyone can figure this out, it's you. But Sage..."

"Yes?"

"Promise me something. Talk to Freddy and the Charming Four. Maybe you can stay here with Freddy when they are gone on missions. I wouldn't be surprised if the crowned prince showed up last night specifically because he knew they were gone. You're not safe."

"I promise. I'll talk to Freddy and the Charming Four today." She hugged her friend and then took another sip of her coffee. "I guess I better get going and find that book. Wish me luck!"

Piper hugged her and gave her a warm smile before heading back to the cafe downstairs.

Sage wandered to the shelves of ancient texts, feeling more energized after speaking with Piper. She scanned the books as she walked, her gaze sweeping from one spine to another. After what seemed like hours, she finally spotted a promising book. It was an old tome with a tattered cover and faded lettering on the spine that read *Magical Medicinal Uses of Honey*.

Excitement coursed through Sage's veins as she gently pulled the book from its resting place. She ran her fingers along the soft leather cover before carefully opening it. Detailed illustrations and long passages about honey and its various uses in medicine throughout history filled the pages. It was precisely what Sage had been searching for.

As Sage flipped through the pages, taking in all the information, something shifted within her. This was it; this book held the secrets to unlocking her theory about how to cure Freddy and Prince Finn's curse.

***

When Freddy and Sage reached the Charming Four's mansion, the gates were open, and light filled the windows. The grounds were bustling with activity as servants hustled about their business carrying packages of all sizes. Sage could feel the tension in the air. Something was going on.

They walked up the cobblestone path, and Sage looked up at the grand manor house. It was beginning to feel like home, something she hadn't expected.

As they walked, they could hear laughter and music coming from the grand hall. They entered the entryway and saw the Charming Four gathered around the fireplace in the sitting room. Relief washed over her, knowing they had returned from their adventure.

Freddy cleared his throat. "Uh, hello?"

The four mages turned to them. Asher looked them up and down. His expression was one of surprise. "It's good to see you're home, Sage. But you," Asher nodded to Freddy, "what are you doing here?"

Before either of them could answer, Sage's eyes dropped. Her heart leaped into her throat.

Colby stepped forward. "Sage, are you alright?"

Sage took a deep breath and then began to tell them her story. She described the crown prince's attempt to force her to make poison and how she used mad honey in the tea to make him hallucinate. She finished with how Freddy had shown up, and they altered the potion Prince Owen had her make.

The four were silent. "Sage, this is serious," Sawyer finally said.

Asher placed his hands on Sage's shoulders. "I'm glad you're safe." The others nodded.

"We all are. You have shown yourself to be resourceful. We need to figure out what to do next, though. If Owen already has her in his sight, it's dan- gerous for all of us."

Sage nodded. "I understand."

Sawyer smiled at her. "We will figure something out. Don't worry. We will protect you."

Freddy put his hand on her shoulder. "I'll do what I can to help, too."

Sage smiled. She was relieved to know that she had the support of her friends.

"She should come with us," Prince Finn said.

"On your missions?" Freddy asked. "She can stay with me while you're gone."

Asher looked at Prince Finn. "That's actually not a bad idea. It would be good to have someone with medical knowledge on some of our missions; we should be able to protect her between the four of us. This next one, she actually would be useful in quite a few ways."

Colby and Sawyer nodded. Sage was confused. She wasn't against traveling with them, but she had no skills to protect herself on the type of missions she imagined they went on.

"Where are you going on your next mission?" she asked.

"The Freefall region," Prince Finn replied. "There's been serious flooding in the area. It's not a guild mission but a request from my father. We will be representing the royal court as part of the relief."

The hustle of servants in the courtyard suddenly made sense. They had been packing relief supplies and readying for the Charming Four.

"When do we leave?" Sage asked.

"First thing tomorrow morning," Prince Finn answered.

"I will need to stop by a shop to restock a few things beforehand. Flooding often causes certain illnesses to run rampant. I should get treatments for the most common ones."

"Whatever you need, honeybee." Prince Finn smirked.

"What did you call me?"

He laughed. "I'm not the one who used honey to poison the future king. I think the name fits."

Sage's face heated. "I didn't poison him."

"Oh?" Sawyer replied, brow raised. "It doesn't take a lethal dose to be considered poison."

"I will have you know that mad honey is used for medicinal purposes by many."

"Whatever you say, honeybee," Prince Finn replied as he headed toward the door. "Pack and get some rest. We leave early."

Sage wasn't impressed with her new nickname, but she was excited to have the opportunity to see a bit more of the world. Travel was something her family hadn't done, and she had accepted the likelihood that she would only ever travel through the eyes of the authors in the books she read.

***

Sage had just stepped out of the Apothecary, her basket filled with the supplies she needed before leaving with the Charming Four. She was regretting not grabbing her cloak. There was just enough nip in the early morning air to raise goosebumps when the wind blew by.

Her steps quickened as she hurried through the nearly empty streets. There was only one last stop she wanted to make before they left. Her nose guided her. The smell of freshly baked bread called to her.

Sage entered a small mom-and-pop bakery. The little bell jangled as Sage stepped inside, announcing her presence. The cozy shop was just large enough for a few tables scattered around the room. Its wood-paned windows were inviting and the sign over the door promised the best pastries in town.

The little shop was filled with the aromas of warm sweet buns, savory pies, and freshly churned butter. The shelves were lined with dozens of different kinds of breads - white, wheat, rye, oat, and more - as well as baskets of fragrant fruits. It was like stepping into a bakery straight out of a fairytale. There was even a glass case with delicate cakes in all shapes and sizes that looked too perfect to eat.

The baker behind it was busy kneading dough, talking to herself as she worked. Their flour dusted jet black hair was pulled into a tight bun on top of their head, tied with a bright yellow ribbon that matched her apron. Sage couldn't help but smile at the sight. The woman looked up from her work and smiled back when she noticed her standing there, eyes darting among all the treats on display.

"Sage!"

This was the baker's daughter who had taken over the bakery several years ago. Sage had been thrilled when they had been able to start getting their bread from here again.

She smiled widely and waved.

"Good morning, Sarina," Sage said. "It's been a while since I've seen you."

"Yes, it has. How have you been? I heard your mother's latest book is out."

"It is," Sage said with a nod. "I think it's going to be a hit. How are things at the bakery?"

"Oh, they're going well. Business has been good. Really good, actually," Sarina said. "I'm glad you stopped by. What can I get you?"

"Do you have any potato bread ready?"

"I do! Fresh out of the oven. How many?"

Sage placed her basket on the counter. "Fill me up. I thought I'd pick some up for the rest of my companions. We've been traveling for a while and I thought it would be nice to share some bread with them."

Sarina nodded in understanding. "That's a nice gesture. I'm sure they will appreciate it."

Sage couldn't help but ask, "Is there anything new you've baked that I could try? I'm feeling a little adventurous today."

Sarina's eyes lit up with excitement. "Actually, I've been working on a new recipe. It's for a cherry and almond pastry. It's still experimental, but I'd love it if you could try it and let me know what you think."

Sage's mouth watered at the thought of it. "I would love to try it."

Sarina quickly disappeared into the back of the bakery and returned with a small plate. She placed it in front of Sage and watched as she took a bite. Sage closed her eyes to savor the flavors. The sweetness of the cherries and the nuttiness of the almonds were a perfect combination.

"This is amazing, Sarina. You should definitely add it to your menu."

Sarina smiled. "Thank you, Sage. I'm glad you like it."

Sage admired the baked goods as Sarina began to pull the loaves of bread, taking in all the delicious smells around her. She had always loved the peaceful atmosphere of the bakery and the comforting smells that came with it. It reminded her of home, of a simpler time when she had no worries or responsibilities.

Her thoughts were interrupted as the door to the bakery swung open, causing the little bell to chime once again. Sage turned to see who had entered and her heart skipped a beat when she saw him. It was the last person she had expected to see there.

"Prince Finn!"

Prince Finn looked at Sage with a curious expression on his face. "Are you almost finished here? Everyone is waiting on us."

Sage was taken aback by his sudden appearance. She had assumed he was preparing his own things for their journey. How did he know where to find her? "Ah-um...y-yes," she stammered as she grabbed her basket of bread off the counter. "I just wanted to pick up some bread."

Prince Finn nodded and gestured for her to lead the way. Ignoring the look of surprise on Sarina's face, Sage waved goodbye and made her way to the exit.

As they began walking back, Sage glanced over at him from time to time, noting how relaxed he looked. He still carried an aura of power and authority, but there was also something softer about him now.

She wasn't sure she was ready to admit why exactly, but she couldn't help but steal glances at him as they walked through the empty streets. He was tall and lean, with piercing brown eyes that seemed to see right through her. His long black hair was perfectly styled, but there was a hint of stubble on his chin that made him look rugged and handsome.

"You seem awfully quiet," Prince Finn said, breaking the silence. Sage jumped a little, surprised by his words. "Are you feeling nervous about the journey?"

Sage swallowed hard, trying to compose herself. "A little, I suppose," she admitted. "I've never been on a mission like this before. I haven't really traveled much. I hope I'll be able to keep up with you and the others."

Prince Finn smiled reassuringly. "Don't worry. Your skills I'm sure will be put to good use and any surprises that come up you've got us. It's not a one sided situation going on here."

Sage nodded, still feeling uncertain. "Thank you. By the way, how did you know where to find me?"

"By chance actually. I was heading to the apothecary you frequent to look for you and happened to see you through the window."

Before she could ask him any more questions, a loud yell cut through the air and they both turned towards it. Sage's heart jumped into her throat as she saw a large boar charging towards them, followed closely by a frantic man chasing after it.

Prince Finn acted fast and grabbed her, his flames whipping up around them, raising them above the animal as it ran by. Sage gasped at the sudden jolt of energy that surged through her body as they hovered in midair. She could feel her cheeks flush as she felt the heat radiating from him and quickly averted her eyes, not wanting to appear too forward.

Prince Finn gently lowered them back onto the ground and released his hold on Sage. His face was unreadable but his eyes were burning with intensity. "Are you okay?" he asked quietly.

Sage nodded mutely, still unable to find words that would adequately express how she was feeling at that moment. She couldn't remember the last time someone had taken such quick action to protect her like that. No, she was pretty sure nothing like that had ever happened before.

"We should keep moving," Prince Finn said after a few moments of silence had passed between them. He offered his arm to Sage, who hesitantly took it

and allowed him to lead her down the street once
more.

***

The sun shone brightly as Prince Finn and Sage
rode in the carriage to the Freefall region. Escorted
by a troop of the king's soldiers to assist in the relief
they were bringing, their entourage stretched long
behind them.

Sage was dressed in her simplest white dress, a
red apron pinned to the front and sat comfortably against the well-padded cushion of her seat. In
her hands was *the* book—an ancient tome detailing
honey's many magical medicinals. As the carriage
jostled along the bumpy road, Sage read intently,
admiring the descriptions of a reclusive guild of
apothecaries in the Freefall region.

Prince Finn was a silent companion. She almost
wished she was in the carriage with Asher, Sawyer,
and Colby, but she wouldn't complain about the
opportunity to read uninterrupted.

The scenery outside was constantly shifting as
they made their journey. Sage watched the sun dip
low in the sky with a wistful sigh, casting its golden
glow on the far-off hills and forests. In the distance,
a small lake glistened in the light, beckoning them to
come closer. But the road curved away before they
could reach it, leading them to the next town.

As the sun sank even lower, Sage was captivated by the endless beauty surrounding them. They passed through fields of wildflowers, their petals swaying in the breeze. They crossed a bridge that seemed to span an entire valley and go on forever. Sage gazed at the tall trees that stood sentry over the landscape, their branches reaching out like arms to embrace the twilight sky.

"It's beautiful," she mumbled.

"It is."

Prince Finn's voice startled her. She didn't realize she had said it out loud.

"Tomorrow, we will begin to enter the affected area. We will stay at an inn and make short day trips from there."

Unsure what she could add to that, she merely nodded, staying silent instead.

The night was filled with the chirps of frogs and crickets and the rustle of trees as the night slowly passed. Sage could not help but marvel at the awe-inspiring views that filled her vision. She wished the journey would never end, for one could never experience the beauty of the world around her in a single lifetime.

Soon, the stars twinkled like an infinite number of diamonds spread across the night sky. Sage was mesmerized and could not help but feel a sense of wonder at all the beauty surrounding her.

The stars seemed to guide them on their journey, and soon enough, a small town rose around them.

The carriage stopped in front of an inn, and the door opened.

Prince Finn exited the carriage, his broad shoulders blocking most of the sunset. Sage scooted to the door and, book in hand, attempted to follow him. Her leg cramped as she stood, and before she could regain her balance, Prince Finn had already caught her in his arms.

The warmth of his embrace was comforting, and Sage melted into it as he gently set her on the ground. He looked deeply into her eyes with a certain twinkle that made her heart skip a beat. The moment seemed to stretch on for an eternity before Prince Finn smirked and stepped away, leaving Sage feeling both relieved and disappointed at the same time.

"Let's go, honeybee," he said with a mischievous glint in his eye.

Sage nodded, blushing slightly as she followed him into the inn.

The rest of the Charming Four entered the inn with them settled at a table near the wall.

A heavy-set woman approached with a curious expression

"Welcome.What can I get for you all this evening?"

Sage let the others do the ordering while she looked around at her surroundings. Colorful tapestries that depicted stories from long ago and intricate wooden carvings lined the walls. She could feel centuries of history seeping out from every corner of the inn as if time had been frozen.

The woman returned shortly after with a large spread of food, enough for each one to sample. A roast chicken with herbs tucked into the crispy skin. Potatoes, freshly baked bread, various fresh vegetables, a small jar of honey, and mugs of local mead.

Sage inhaled the food's aroma, savoring each scent and feeling her hunger rise.

"It smells heavenly. Thank you," Sage said to the woman.

"Of course! We appreciate the help you are all bringing. We've prepared the two rooms reserved. They are the first on the left up the stairs." The woman offered a warm smile before retreating to the kitchen.

They all dug into the food, discussing their journey and speculating what would come next.

After dinner, everyone agreed it was time for bed and began making their way up to their rooms on the second floor.

Sage hesitated once they reached the top of the stairs. A glance in both rooms and she realized that her last-minute addition to their party would cause a problem for their lodging situation.

"Where are the rest of the soldiers and help sleeping? Perhaps they have a spare tent I can sleep in," Sage said to no one in particular.

"All the tents have been taken," Prince Finn said, stepping forward before the others could reply.

"The soldiers and help will sleep outside. You will sleep in my room." Prince Finn's voice was firm and left no room for argument.

Sage glanced at Asher before she nodded and followed him into the room.

The room was small, with only one bed and a chair in the corner. But it was tidy and clean and more than comfortable for the two of them.

Sage settled into the chair, carefully keeping her distance from the bed and Prince Finn. He watched her silently as he moved to the bed, pulling the blanket off.

"Are you planning on sleeping in the chair?"

She thought of her initial plans to sleep in the library closet. "I've had worse options before. I can sleep on the floor if I get too uncomfortable."

He rolled his eyes. "I will not lay a hand on you. We need you well rested, and the floor is drafty. There's only one blanket. You will be of no help if you get sick."

Her heart raced. He couldn't be serious, could he?

He removed his shoes and stripped down to only his pants and an undershirt.

"I promise to be nothing but a gentleman," he said, patting the bed beside him. "Would you prefer the wall or the edge?"

Sage swallowed hard. Taking a deep breath and releasing it slowly, she decided to trust him. He hadn't proven to her that she couldn't, as much as he had driven her crazy, and at the moment, her only other options were even less desirable.

"Wall, please."

He nodded and gestured for her to take the other side of the bed.

Sage hesitantly moved to the bed and lay down.

"Goodnight, Sage," he said softly.

"Goodnight." She was more than aware of every movement Prince Finn made, but she managed to drift off to sleep in the end.

The Freefall Flooding

Heavy gusts of wind blew across the ruined farmland, the dry cracked ground giving way to damp, muddy pathways. Sage followed without fail, her eyes darting from one flooded building to the next, her heart heavy. The once-majestic homes and barns that had spanned the valleys' great expanse were now little more than broken twisted husks of their former selves.

Everything was coated in a thick layer of mud and debris, a grim reminder of the destruction that had come to pass. Even the sky seemed heavy with grief. The dark, ominous clouds that were once welcomed as a sign of life were now a reminder of the material losses suffered.

A lump began forming in her throat, her sadness deepening with each step. They walked in a solemn line, their faces grim and determined as they made their way toward the relief camp on the hill. The only dry spot for several miles.

The Charming Four and the soldiers were comforting, their silent but steady presence a reminder that hope remained no matter the darkness surrounding them. In the distance, people laughed. The familiar sound brought a measure of solace, and the grief felt a little less heavy.

Sage kept her gaze fixed, her eyes determinedly forward, her bag of medicine a comforting weight against her side. Her muddy skirts weighed her down, and each step took great effort the closer she got to the camp, but it was all worth it.

They were bringing hope.

Soon she reached the hilltop, and the sight warmed and broke her heart at the same time. It was clear that these people had lost everything. The floods had come quickly, and very few had made it out with more than the clothes on their backs.

Soldiers with food had arrived before her, and small groups gathered to eat their first meals in several days. While this was a devastating moment, she saw smiles on most of the peoples' faces.

Sage swallowed the lump in her throat, and she let the tears of relief wash over her face. She closed her eyes, her heavy heart lightening and her body exhausted, and when she opened them again, she felt a strange sense of peace.

She turned to Asher beside her. "Where do you need me?" she asked, her voice barely above a whisper.

Asher smiled at her, a touch of gratitude in his eyes. "We need you in the medical tent over there. You can help prepare potions and remedies to help people heal and recover."

Sage nodded, her determination renewed. "I'm ready."

Asher smiled again, his shoulders relaxing slightly. "Thank you."

With that, Sage set off to do her part. For the next few hours, she worked tirelessly, mixing and preparing potions and remedies that she hoped would help those in need. With luck, her meager knowledge would make a difference in the lives of those who had lost so much.

She mixed herbs and roots with a practiced hand, adding lavender oil to soothe headaches, chamomile for upset stomachs, calendula for minor cuts and scrapes, and sage for respiratory relief. Sage prayed it would help those who needed it most with every potion she made.

When the sun had set and the medical tent was quiet, Sage stepped out into the night air and looked around. Promise and hope filled the camp, and it was clear that the people were determined to rebuild their lives.

Sage smiled, feeling a swell of pride and joy in her heart. She had done her part to bring a little relief to those in need.

As she turned to leave, she felt a gentle hand on her shoulder and looked up to see Asher.

"It's late. Should we head back?" she asked him.

"We should stay here tonight. The others headed back earlier and will return with more supplies. It's not safe for us to try and make our way back in the dark."

Sage nodded and looked around. "I guess we should find a spot by a fire to stay warm tonight. Who knew Prince Finn's ability would be so useful in a mission like this?"

Asher directed her toward a small fire near the camp's outskirts. "It's good for his ego to dry firewood instead of just burning things down."

Sage's laughter echoed in the crisp night air.

They settled in near the fire, the warmth of the flames a comfort in the darkness. Together they watched the stars as they twinkled in the night sky.

"Have you ever thought about what you want your future to look like?" Sage asked.

Asher was silent, his gaze distant as he seemed to consider her question.

"Will you stay a member of the Charming Four or start a family someday?" she persisted.

Asher turned to her and smiled, his eyes twinkling in the firelight. "I'm not sure what I want my future to look like yet," he said softly. "But whatever I do, it will always involve helping others. That's the most important thing." He paused and looked back at the stars. "Maybe one day, though, I'll have fulfilled my duties with the Charming Four and find myself a wife, settle down somewhere near these mountains, and start a family."

Sage looked at him, admiration and respect shining in her eyes. She admired how the firelight reflected off Asher's chestnut-colored hair, the memory of Asher and a mystery woman together in the garden still fresh in her mind.

"I'm sure you will," she said, smiling. "You'll make a wonderful husband and father someday."

Asher returned the smile. "Glad to hear that someone thinks so."

"Would you ever want to do both? I mean, stay in the Charming Four and have a family?"

His gaze turned to the fire. "It's a possibility. If she agreed and the others did as well. I don't know if that's possible, though."

"Why not?"

With a heavy sigh, Asher picked up a stick and poked at the hot coals, "There's ... someone. I mean, I have someone I like, but the way things currently are, it's not... We aren't possible."

"I'm sorry to hear that," Sage said, her heart aching for him. She wanted to reach out and take his hand in comfort but felt it would be too familiar.

"Don't be. I can't make a promise to her that I'm not sure I can keep. I don't want to disappoint her when I can't be there for her."

Sage listened to the sound of the crackling fire as it slowly died down. She looked at the sky, the stars still twinkling in the night.

She felt a calmness wash over her. "Whatever you decide, I'm sure it will be the right decision."

Asher nodded and offered her a small smile. "Thank you. I hope so."

The two of them sat in comfortable silence for the rest of the night, their future hopes and dreams lingering in the air.

***

The moon was a sliver of silver in the night sky, its feeble light barely able to penetrate the thick blanket of fog that shrouded the countryside. Sage stirred in her sleep, her body waking to a small voice calling her name. She opened her eyes to the darkness, suddenly aware of the child beside her.

"Please, you must come with me," he said. His voice was small, trembling, and his eyes were wide with fear. "My mother is very ill and I need your help. Please."

Sage sat up and looked around the small camp. Asher lay sleeping beside her, undisturbed. She sensed that she had to act quickly.

She threw her cloak off her and pulled it over her shoulders, then stood and walked away from the dying embers of their fire to where the boy stood waiting. He was a small frail thing, his clothes thin and his eyes full of tears.

"Where is your mother?"

"Just beyond the trees," he said, pointing in the general direction of the woods.

Sage studied the boy, her heart aching for his fear and sorrow. He had no one else to turn to and she was his only hope. With a deep breath, she nodded and followed him into the receding flooded forest.

The air was chilly and thick with fog, the mist clinging to her skin like a thin layer of ice. She shivered as she walked, the boy close beside her, his hand gripping hers as if it were his only anchor.

The forest was dark and silent, and it seemed like they were the only two creatures alive in the world. The trees loomed above them like silent sentinels, and an owl hooted in the distance.

They reached a clearing, and the boy pointed out a small hut. Leaves thatched the roof and large, dark-brown stones made up the structure's walls. A window on each side and an open door with a small, smokeless fire. The moon above peeked through the clouds and reflected off the puddles in the mud surrounding the home.

Sage stepped forward, her feet sinking deep into the mud. She hesitated, her heart pounding, before pushing open the door.

Inside, the hut was dark, only lit by moonlight. A woman lay on a bed, her skin pale and breathing shallow. Sage could see that she was deathly ill.

She knelt beside the woman and touched her face, tears stinging her eyes.

"Please," a whisper broke the silence. "Help me," the woman said.

Sage nodded and began pulling bottles and cloth from her bag. She prepared a potion of willow bark to break the fever and help her recover, adding a few drops of lavender oil for its calming properties. She then made an ointment of honey and garlic to help alleviate pain before finally making a healing salve of yarrow and olive leaf. She applied all these remedies topically.

Sage stayed with the woman through the night, massaging them into her skin, changing her bandages, and ensuring she was kept as comfortable as possible and could sleep peacefully.

By morning, the fever had broken, and Sage knew the woman would recover fully.

The woman smiled weakly at them both. "Thank you," she said softly. "You have saved my life."

Sage blushed under the woman's gaze and nodded. Without her help, this stranger would have died in this tiny hut lost in an ancient forest. She thanked the gods for guiding her here and giving her the courage to help a stranger in need even though she was so far from home.

The woman glanced around the hut before turning back to Sage, her eyes brightening with hope. "Will you stay here for a while?" she asked hesitantly. "There is not much I can offer you, but I can tell you stories of our guild if you'd like. I assume the honey you used to treat me is of the average variety?"

"It was. It's great for treating burns, sore throats and can help with pain among other things." Sage smiled, feeling strangely drawn to this mysterious place and its inhabitants. She was sure many tales had been hidden within these walls, tales of love and loss but also strength and courage—stories of ordinary people doing extraordinary things when faced with adversity.

The woman motioned for her son to join her on the small bed, and Sage settled on a chair nearby.

"Very true. Did you know that some honey can do even more though? The first time I heard about the secret magic of honey," the woman began, "was from my grandmother. She told me stories of a reclusive guild of mages hidden deep in the forest, living in a beautiful, elegant garden. According to her, these mages could create powerful potions with magical honey as the key ingredient. It was a secret only the locals knew about, and even they gave it a wide berth.

"At the time, I didn't believe such a thing was possible, but my grandmother's stories stayed with me, and I eventually found myself searching for the guild in the forest. After days of wandering, I stumbled across this garden. I was amazed at its beauty. Everywhere I looked were vibrant flowers, buzzing bees, and many plants I couldn't imagine existing anywhere else.

"As I approached, a figure stepped out of the shadows. It was an old man with a long white beard and deep blue eyes. He introduced himself as the guild's leader. He explained that the magical honey was created through a complex process involving the tending of bees and carefully harvesting rare and precious flowers. He said the potions created from these kinds of honey could heal any wound or illness and even bring life back to the dead."

Sage's mind drifted to the book she had borrowed from the library. It seemed plausible that this could be the same group, and the promise of bringing life back to the dead made her hopeful that she could possibly use it to help cure the gargoyle curse.

"He then told me about a woman who had been close to death but was brought back to life through the guild's potion. I was filled with awe and admiration for this guild, and I couldn't help but marvel at the power of their secret magic.

"The old man then offered to let me join. I eagerly accepted. I learned the guild's secrets and tended to the bees and flowers in their garden. Over time, I understood the true power of the honey. I have witnessed many miracles. It is a magical thing, one that I would never trade for anything in the world."

"You're a member of the guild?" Sage asked.

The woman coughed. Sage offered a drink from her flask of fresh water, which the woman eagerly swallowed.

"I was. I met my husband there. The poor man passed a year ago from a mix-up while testing a new honey. After that, I needed some space, so we moved here. It's quiet and a good place to raise a child."

"Do you ever miss it or wish you could go back?"

The woman chuckled. "Who says we don't? It's not far. We visit when the weather is good."

Sage knew she should head back to the camp, but this was an opportunity she feared wouldn't happen again.

"May I ask why your son came to find me instead of going to the guild?"

"It's far," the boy answered. "I was afraid I wouldn't get back in time. Ma needed help, and people passing by told me a healer would be at the camp."

"Clever boy. How did you know that I was the healer?"

His eyes darted to her bag. "I could smell the potions you carry."

The woman looked at her son warmly. "He's got his father's nose."

"You have a very brave and resourceful son."

"Thank you," the woman whispered.

Sage rose and looked at the boy, smiling.

"I should go now," she said, handing him a small medicine bag to continue treating his mother. "When she is strong enough, you should head to the camp. I would like to check in on you so we can find help to clean up the damage to your home." Sage picked up her bag and hesitated. "Can I ask how I could find your guild? I know they prefer to stay secret, but I have a few people for whom I am looking for treatment, and I'm at a loss."

The woman studied Sage before nodding and pointing out a window to the west. "Almost a day's walk that way, you will find it. It's at the top of a cliff, so they should have avoided the flooding. It's easy to miss, though. If you reach the cliffside, follow it away from here, and you will find it. Tell them Rosey sent you."

"And Thomas!" the boy piped in.

Sage laughed as she walked toward the door. "I will do that. Thank you. When you check in at the camp, can you tell someone where I went? Look for any member of the Charming Four."

"You ensured that my son didn't become an orphan. It's the least I can do."

Sage bowed her head, touched by the woman's kindness, and thanked her once more before departing.

As Sage made her way back through the forest, she thought about what the woman had said. Not only did the guild hold the key to healing the gargoyle curse, but it also seemed to offer a safe refuge from the outside world. She wondered what other secrets the guild was hiding and why it had chosen to remain hidden for so long.

***

Sage stood at the cliff's edge, watching the sun dip beneath the horizon. The sky was awash with shades of pink, orange, and blue, the twilight casting a soft glow over the landscape. All around her was a blanket of tranquility. And in the distance, a garden unlike anything she had seen before. Even the castle garden seemed insignificant compared to this.

It sparkled in the dying light, beckoning her forward, and her feet crunched on the dry grass. In the last hour or so, she had risen above the mud from the flood and was so grateful.

As she drew closer, she could make out the intricate shapes of the hedges and the bright flowers. The garden had been carefully tended to as if it were a living work of art.

Sage stepped into the garden, her eyes taking in its beauty. Her heart raced with anticipation, for she knew she was getting closer to the secret guild. She meandered through the winding paths, taking in the sights. Statues of beautiful goddesses and gods carefully crafted from the finest marble. Smaller statues depicted scenes of everyday life as if someone had taken the time to create a miniature version of the world.

The statues were life-like, but even the best sculptor couldn't capture a person's movements or their personality. At least, her father had always said that. But here ... in this garden ... you could see a deer at the edge of the woods. In its eyes, a hint of fear as it caught sight of you. Sage had a hard time imagining that the deer was, in fact, a statue.

She noted a beehive near one of the statues and a man looking back at a giant as he ran across a narrow stone bridge.

Red flowers surrounded her, with waves of blue, yellow, green, and purple visible glowing in the distance. They swayed with the wind, like the goddess' hair flowing in the breeze. A butterfly flew through the flowers, adding a blue streak to their red glow.

Sage heard a noise. It was faint, but it was enough to catch her attention. Her eyes scanned the darkness for any movement. After a few moments, she saw a figure standing in the shadows. She could just make out the shape of a man, his face hidden by a hood. He did not move, and Sage realized he had been waiting for her.

She took a deep breath, trying to steady her racing heart. She had found the guild, and it was time to enter. With one final glance at the man, she stepped forward, determined to help her friends.

The man met her halfway, his face still hidden in the shadows. "Welcome, you've traveled far to find us," he said, in a low whisper.

Sage nodded, her throat tightening. "I did. How did you know?"

He pointed at her cloak. "Locals use a different type of wool for their cloaks. One treated with a blend from our garden to make it more waterproof. How can we help you, traveler?"

Sage's doubts rose to the surface. She had no idea who this man was or if she could trust him. But, at the same time, she had come too far to turn back now.

"I am looking for help," she said after taking a deep breath. "A treatment for several of my friends." The man slowly nodded as he listened to her words. "I'm an apothecary and haven't found anything yet."

She showed her bag of herbs, remedies, and other concoctions she had collected.

"I may be able to help you find a treatment for your friends," he said, seeming to understand her plight, "but it will take some work on your part. Are you willing?"

Sage swallowed hard before nodding. This would not be an easy task, but it was worth it if it meant saving her friends' lives. With newfound determination, Sage followed the man into the garden's depths. It seemed silly to call it a garden. It was massive. Now that she was deep within it, she could see how it stretched in three directions and disappeared over hills.

Soon they approached a hilltop in the middle of the garden where a small village hid. Sage took in the view as the last light from the sun disappeared, and stars emerged in waves like candles lit at a wedding.

Wooden and stone homes lined several streets, meeting in the center at a pergola and grassy space. Streets cobbled and packed hard from years of use. Several large buildings stood at each corner.

What surprised her was the high level of craftsmanship. Each home seemed to be made by a master carpenter, the wood not just cut and nailed together but given more artistic touches.

The hooded figure stopped and turned to Sage, gesturing for her to enter one of them. Taking a deep breath, Sage entered.

Several people filled the large hall, all wearing dirt-covered clothing and many with smudges still on their hands and faces. Most were seated at communal tables, while a few stood around the edges, talking quietly. Sage could feel their eyes on her and sense the curiosity in their gaze.

As she moved into the room, the hooded figure weaved through the crowd. Sage followed close behind, afraid she might lose him. He stopped before a woman in a green dress with muddy brown boots. Her salt-and-pepper, curly hair was pulled back into a long braid, keeping her face clear, reminding Sage of an acorn in both shade and shape. She held a gentle yet regal air, her gaze piercing and all-knowing.

"Rachel, we have a visitor," the hooded man said as he pulled off his cloak to reveal a middle-aged man with wavy black hair pulled back low.

Rachel's gaze moved from the man to Sage, and a small smile appeared.

"Welcome. I'm Rachel, the leader of Nectars Embrace. This is Michael. We are a mage group specializing in healing and protection magic."

"Sage. My name is Sage. Sorry, I'm a bit off. Rosey and Thomas told me how to find you."

"Oh? We haven't seen them for some time. I hope they are well." Rachel gestured to a table nearby while Michael left them alone.

Sage followed Rachel and sat across from her.

"The lower area has been badly flooded, and I came with the king's representatives to assist.

Thomas found me in the camp and brought me to his mother. To be honest, if he didn't, I'm afraid she would probably be no longer of this world."

Rachel nodded in understanding. "Your magic is weak, and yet you are here. It is a testament to your courage. I know it may seem strange to you, but if you are here, you must have something to offer. May I ask what brings you to us?"

"You can tell all that about me already? We just met."

"You don't get to be the leader of a guild such as this without some unique skills. Being able to read people's magical ability is one of mine."

"Is there anything else you read off me?"

"Only a little. You don't have an affinity for any particular magic, but if you trained correctly, you would be able to read the magic of others in a similar way that I do. I can teach you if you would like."

"That would be fantastic!" Sage said with a clap of her hands.

"What's fantastic?" Michael asked as he placed two plates full of roasted vegetables and crusty bread on the table. One in front of himself and one in front of Sage.

"Your friend here appears to have a similar ability to read magic as I do."

Michael's smile made his eyes twinkle. "That is fantastic! Very few people can do that."

All the attention was making Sage squirm a bit. She picked up a piece of bread and took a bite. It was soft and still warm. Her stomach growled as if it were offering its approval and encouragement for more.

"So tell us, why did you seek us out?"

Sage brushed crumbs from the corner of her mouth. "I'm looking for a treatment for several friends. I know of none and saw mention of your guild in a book. I was hoping you may have something or at least would be willing to work with me to try and figure one out."

"Just what are we trying to heal?" Michael asked.

"Gargoyles."

Rachel leaned forward on her elbows. "Just what do you know about gargoyles? It's not a topic that is spoken of lightly."

"I agree. A ... a friend of mine has the affliction. Late set, while another is in the early stages. Have you ever treated one?"

The corner of Rachel's mouth twitched. "No, but I do love a good challenge. Tell me everything you know."

As they ate, Sage shared everything she had learned so far.

Michael and Rachel listened intently, only interrupting to ask clarifying questions.

Once she finished, Rachel leaned back in her chair, her brow furrowed in thought.

"It sounds like you have a strong grasp on what's happening with these two, but I'm not sure there is a cure. We may be able to slow down the progression, but there is no guarantee."

Michael nodded. "The good news is that we are Nectars Embrace. We specialize in creating and finding cures in ways that no one else would think of. We'll do all we can to help."

Sage felt hope fill her. "Thank you both so much."

"No need to thank us. We're happy to help," Rachel said, smiling. First, let's get you settled somewhere for the night, and we can get a fresh start in the morning. Rosey's place is still empty. You are welcome to stay there if you would like."

"That sounds perfect."

Michael picked up their plates and motioned for her to follow him. After depositing them on a table at the back of the room with other dirty dishes, he guided her out to the streets.

"You can get all your meals in the dining hall. Breakfast at sunrise and dinner at sunset. Usually, there's some sort of fresh snack that you can grab during the day if you need something else."

"That's good to know. Thank you," Sage replied.

Soon they stood at the heavy wooden door of a small cobblestone cottage. Michael reached above the frame and pulled down a small key before using it to unlock the door. He turned around, placed the key in her hand, and motioned for her to enter.

"We don't really have problems with crime in our little community, but if you have any concerns feel free to lock up. Candles are in the kitchen cabinets, blankets and linens in the chest at the foot of each bed, and you can find firewood and the well behind your house. Do you need anything else? Rosey left just about everything behind. Said it was full of memories she couldn't bear to take with her."

Sage looked around the small four-room space and shook her head no. "I think that's everything I need."

With a small smile and nod, he left her alone to explore the space.

Rosey's quaint living room had white plaster coating the walls, and an array of hand-stitched pillows lay atop the aged furniture that had been well taken care of.

Her gaze shifted to the shelves that lined a nearby wall, bursting with books on a variety of topics. She longed to curl up in one corner and delve into their contents, but she needed rest after traveling and instead decided it would be best to tuck in for the night and explore in the morning.

She made her way through the hallway, checking which bedroom looked the most inviting before slipping into the cozy space she would call home for a while. She quickly made the bed and stripped down to her undergarments, snuggling beneath the blanket of feathers as she let out a contented sigh.

The moonlight streamed through the window, bathing everything in its soft glow. Sage lay there letting her thoughts drift over her situation. As she drifted off, only one thought filled her mind—to-

morrow was a new day, full of possibilities waiting
to be explored.

***

In the garden, Sage took a slow, deep breath, in-
haling the heady scents of the late summer flowers.
Rachel was right behind her, with a wide grin, her
deep brown eyes taking in the sights. A moment of
deep peace settled over Sage as the sun shone on
her, and the colorful flowers brightened her vision.

"It's incredible, isn't it?" Rachel asked."I had no idea
I would find this when I stumbled on your guild.
There was nothing of it in my book."

"Sometime you should show me this book. Very
few know of our existence. We use alternate names
for most of our sales, and locals know to keep things
quiet. Many have family here or are descendants
from those who chose to leave."

This section of the garden was lush with a wide
variety of flowers and herbs in full bloom. At the
center was a large statue of a beautiful woman playing with two small children. The woman looked
serene as she held her delicate hands out, reaching
for them. Beside the statue, Sage noticed a beehive
with the activity of its inhabitants.

"This place is magical," Sage said, her eyes glittering.

Rachel nodded. "Yes, it is."

"Does the statue mean anything? I noticed another one yesterday that also had a hive nearby."

Rachel smiled and gestured to the hive. "We name the new breeds of bees after members of our community at that time. That's Enola Draqium. She was a midwife who first noticed that certain plants worked for specific magical abilities and harmed others," she said, her gaze on the beehive and expression thoughtful.

"Wait, how do you mean?"

She pointed at a small red flower with a long stem similar to a poppy. "Take that flower. *Magnetra's ophilium's* healing abilities are amplified with fire mages but hinder healing for ice mages. All the plants around here work like that. The Draqium bees are also attuned best to fire-based magic. It's why they are near each other."

"So everything you've planted has been completely intentional."

"Exactly. Draquim bees are aggressive, and if their hive is too close to another one, they will rob other hives of their honey, potentially spreading or contracting diseases. They are one of the easiest to crossbreed, which we took into account when deciding where to place them. For each new breed, we have to figure out how far they will travel and what their preferences and behaviors are. This was once a small community, but we have spread out over the years, covering a large area of land."

Rachel knelt beside the flower and plucked a tiny sprout. An idea formed in the back of Sage's mind but not quite in full shape.

"Do you want to help? If you see anything that looks like this, we need to pull it. They are seedlings of Sacred Dewberry, best used for ice mages. The seeds sometimes get carried on the wind or dropped from bird droppings as they fly over. We must remove them, or it will tamper with the Draqium bees' honey."

Sage knelt, the soil slightly damp beneath her hands as she pulled up small weeds that had sprung up along the hive's edge. She worked slowly and methodically, her brow furrowed in concentration as she plucked the weeds and tossed them in a small pile beside her.

Rachel worked just as diligently, although her hands moved a bit faster than Sage's. They worked together in quiet companionable silence, and soon they had cleared the weeds in a wide circle around the hive.

When they were finished, they stood and looked at the statue, their work visible in the weed-free area around it. Rachel smiled in appreciation, and Sage nodded in satisfaction.

"That feels like a job well done," Rachel said.

Sage's gaze was on the statue. "It really does."

They took in the garden's beauty before Rachel smiled and pointed to the beehive.

"We should leave the bees in peace now. Come, we will find another area that needs tending before getting lunch."

***

The setting sun's light streamed through the storage room's window, casting a warm glow. Three days had passed since Sage's arrival in the village, and while she hadn't figured out how to solve Freddy and Prince Finn's gargoyle problem, an idea was starting to form.

Sage and Rachel worked in comfortable silence, sorting through the various herbs collected that day. She had begun to recognize the different breeds of plants and bees unique to this guild's work and had come to learn the importance of this small storage room.

The herbs were incredibly valuable. Every day, Sage and Rachel sorted and stored the plants, ready for the apothecaries to use in their various concoctions. Sage couldn't help but feel a sense of pride knowing that the remedies they created here could help people from all walks of life. She understood why her father had chosen this career better now than ever before.

The two women worked in comfortable silence, Sage taking care to label each herb and Rachel ensuring that she securely stored the herbs.

Every few minutes, Sage would pause to breathe in the herbs' sweet fragrant aroma. Rosemary, lavender, thyme, and sage were abundant, and each gave off a unique scent that was both calming and invigorating. It made her think of home.

Sage carefully gathered powdered lavender, lovage root, rosemary leaves and mixed them in a mortar and pestle. The resulting paste was a vibrant green hue, and Sage applied it to her wrists with a careful hand, feeling the coolness immediately take effect. She tinkered with other combinations, testing whether the right mix could relieve various ailments. But sometimes, her experiments yielded unexpected results.

Something caught Sage's eye. A spark of light had appeared in the corner of the room and drew Sage over where she discovered a small silver box tucked away in the shadows.

Sage opened the box and was surprised to find a small vial of golden liquid. She held the vial up to the light. The liquid glowed, seeming to come alive in her hands.

"What is this?" she asked as she removed the vial's stopper, and a pleasant smell filled the storage room, reminding her of the herbs she'd been sorting earlier, honey and something she couldn't quite place.

Rachel walked over and took the small bottle.

"It's an elixir ... or at least, we hope it will be."

Sage's eyes widened with surprise. "An elixir? What would it do?"

Rachel smiled and gestured for Sage to follow her. She walked to the far side of the room and pulled down a drying bundle of shadow lily. She placed the petals in a small bowl and dripped a few drops of the elixir. The black petals began to glow and soon smoked but didn't burn.

"This is what makes this elixir so unique," she explained, pointing to the golden liquid inside the vial. "If we can get this elixir just right, it should act like an amplifier for mages. This was specifically created from the Draqium bee honey surrounded by fire-magic-enhancing plants such as shadow lily, *Magnetra's ophillium*, and silent holly. When a fire mage adds their magic, it becomes more potent over time."

"Do you think...?" Sage began but paused, lost in thought.

"Yes?"

"What if this is the solution?"

Rachel put the stopper on the bottle and placed it back in the silver box.

"How so?"

"Mages slowly become gargoyles as they use magic beyond their natural ability," Sage said, pacing the room, gently touching different plants as she spoke. "What if it's happening because they need to replenish their magic?"

"A mage does that naturally over time."

"True, but what if pushing too far damages something and it's unable to repair or repairs too slowly and is only damaged more when they use their magic before it's healed?"

"I've never known a powerful mage not to use their magic for an extended amount of time, so it is possible. I'm sure they've tried treating it with things that would help recharge their magic, though."

Sage grabbed a lavender bundle from the table and waved it as she continued to pace. "But do they know what specifically to use? Is it information that is readily available for stronger concoctions? I imagine that to become a gargoyle, you have to go beyond your limits by a significant amount. It would take a lot to help them repair it fully before damaging it again. Do you know if your guild has ever treated someone with this before?"

Rachel shook her head no. "I haven't heard of anyone treating it. It's a tight-lipped secret usually."

"Does this elixir become more powerful over time as more mages add to it?" Sage asked, tapping the silver box with the lavender bundle.

"It does. Very slowly, but it does."

"How many mages work with it?"

"A few. Why?"

Sage's mind raced as everything clicked together. "It's only a theory, but what if the reason no one can identify the type of stone that mages turn into as they transition into a gargoyle is that their magic is different than anyone else's? No two mages have the same kind of magic, and if they are turning into stone because their magic is depleting, it would be fair to say what is left would be a non-powered representation of their magic. After all, you can't separate the magic from the mage."

Rachel picked up the bottle from the box and held the golden liquid in the day's last rays. "So you're thinking because of this, we need to use many of the same types of mages to put magic into it, so there would be a higher chance of it being close to the type of magic they need to recharge. What if it was broken down even further?"

"How so?"

"It would be fair to assume that if this is really the solution, if you categorized the ability into subcategories, it could be better used by mages of the same type. For example, an earth mage whose magic works with soil would not be as compatible with one whose magic focuses more on plants."

She beamed with enthusiasm and clapped her hands together. "Exactly!"

"So, how do we test this?"

Sage smiled wider, her cheeks flushed with excitement. "One of the people I'm treating isn't too far away. He's helping treat the flood victims. We could prepare something and take it to him."

Rachel nodded. "Let's do it. What affinity does he have?"

"Fire. I've not seen him use it much, though. I'm not entirely sure how it would fit into a subcategory."

"Understood. Tonight, I will ask several of the fire mages in the guild to add their magic and try to make it cover most types of mages. Tomorrow we will set out to find your patient."

Returning to the Charming Four

S age held her breath as they approached the edge of the flood-victim relief setup on the hill. They had spent the day walking through only slightly drier mud than Sage had walked through a few days before, and her legs were burning.

Behind her, Michael and Rachel stopped and stared, their eyes wide in shock at the destruction. As they walked through the affected areas, they had become quieter and quieter as it sunk in how badly it had been hit. The swarm of residents on top of the hill walking among the tents and other makeshift shelters made Sage's heart ache again.

Sage turned and squeezed Michael's shoulder, comforting him as best she could.

"Come on," Sage said softly, taking Rachel's hand. "It's looking better than when I was here last. Most people should be on the mend by now. Let's see how we can help, and I will find my patient."

The relief tents were bustling with activity as they entered. The air was thick with the smell of porridge and herbs prepared in makeshift kitchens. People of all ages were helping in whatever way they could at the end of the day.

Sage's gaze lingered on a family surrounded by several others. She recognized Thomas, a grin from ear to ear, kicking a ball with several soldiers and other children. The ball escaped the small circle of players and rolled to a stop in front of Sage. Thomas ran to retrieve it, his face lighting up with excitement when he noticed her presence.

"It's you! You're back!"

His mother, Rosey, pushed through the crowd behind him and gave Sage a warm smile as she reached them. Her gaze lingered on Rachel and Michael, and her eyes widened in surprise.

"I didn't expect you to come personally," Rosey said, her gaze softening. "It's good to see you, old friend."

Rachel's hand rested on Rosey's arm. "It's been far too long."

"If you wouldn't mind," Rosey started as she turned to face the medical tents behind her, "I could use another opinion. An illness I'm unfamiliar with has begun to spread within the camp. I'm assuming it's from close quarters and the mosquitos that have been rampant thanks to the standing water and mud surrounding us."

"Of course," Michael said. "Bring us to them."

Sage glanced around, looking for any member of the Charming Four. "I will catch up with all of you in a few minutes. I have something I need to check in on first."

Rosey laughed. "I bet you do! When I showed up here, the camp had practically been turned upside down, and soldiers were patrolling for you in the mud. A warning would have been nice before you sent me to face one of the princes."

Cheeks burning, Sage offered a pitiful smile. "I'm sorry. I should have thought of that."

Rosey waved away the comment. "It's quite alright. Now go find your traveling companions before I get in trouble for keeping you again."

Sage smiled and said goodbye before turning away. She wandered through the camp, noticing how many more tents had been set up. It felt more like a small city now. Sage spotted Sawyer playing a flute near a fire and stopped to listen, allowing the music to wash over her and fill her with hope. The notes danced in the air, lifting some of the stress from her shoulders.

Sawyer's eyes closed, and his body swayed with each note he played. The beauty of it was almost too much to take in, and Sage found herself reaching out, trying to capture some of that lightness for her own heart.

With an extended final note, a moment of silence hung in the air before those gathered started to clap. Sawyer's eyes opened, and with a small smile, he nodded his thanks until his eyes landed on Sage.

Sawyer stood and made his way over to her. "Look who decided to show up. You couldn't have shown up at a better time. Someone has been extra moody and driving me crazy."

Sage laughed. "Let me guess ... Asher?"

"Him too."

Brow raised, Sage waited for Sawyer to explain, only to be disappointed.

Sawyer started walking further into the camp, with Sage following.

"It appears you have gotten a lot done while I've been gone," Sage offered.

"We have. It's going to be a few weeks before anyone can return home and start cleaning up, so we've tried to make it feel as much like home here as we can. It's had a few unexpected issues arise, but for the most part, people have been patient."

"I heard about the new illness. How bad is it?"

"It's still early," he said after a moment. "Hopefully, we can figure it out soon."

"I understand. I brought some help with me. They may be able to recognize it and offer treatment."

Sawyer nodded. "That's good. I have a feeling we are going to need it. This way."

He led her down the line of tents, past the cooking fire, and around a corner to a secluded area. A large tent had been set up with several people milling about it. Sawyer led her to it and opened the flap, letting her enter first.

Rugs and cushions in soft blues and greens decorated the inside and gave it an airy feel, despite being full of people. Sage spotted Asher and Colby, their eyes wide with surprise as they saw Sage standing unharmed.

"Sage!" Asher cried out in relief as he ran up to hug her tightly. "You're okay! We were so worried about you."

Colby stood beside Sawyer, smirking. "Ran off to have an adventure of your own?"

"Something like that," Sage said with a wink. "I actually have something I needed to give to Prince Finn. Is he here?"

Someone cleared their throat behind Sage. She turned around to find Prince Finn. A twinkle in his eye told her he wasn't as grumpy as he was trying to look.

Sage's heart fluttered at seeing him, even though she was nervous about speaking. Taking a deep breath, she reached into her bag and retrieved a small box wrapped in brown paper and tied with pale blue ribbon.

"Can we go somewhere to talk? I have something I need to show you."

He led her out of the tent without a word before pointing to another one further away. They made their way over and entered, where she found dimly lit candles providing a soft glow.

The inside was much different than what she had seen in the larger tent. Instead of cushions and rugs, large pillows covered portions of the floor with several baskets filled with food provisions and herbs for healing. In one corner was a stack of books indicating that this was probably Prince Finn's tent.

He gestured toward one of the pillows, which Sage accepted gratefully, before pouring two cups of tea into small mugs. An unfamiliar blend hit her nose, and her mouth began to water.

Prince Finn settled on a pillow across from her. His eyes were unreadable. "You wanted to talk to me?"

"I did." Sage set the small package on the table next to her mug. "I found something I want to try as a treatment for you."

A slight look of disappointment flickered on Prince Finn's face before becoming neutral again. "That's why you disappeared?"

Sage sighed, her fingers playing with the small package between them. She had returned for him, for Prince Finn, and for this very moment. Her hands shook, her heart thundered, and her throat felt tight as she tried to find her words.

"I never meant to leave without telling you," she began, her voice gentle like a feather dancing in the wind. "I regret it deeply." Prince Finn nodded, his expression only slightly changing as she spoke. "I never wanted to hurt any of you. I should have at least told Asher what was happening. The boy seemed so desperate, and I was only half awake."

She was sure the members of the Charming Four would have had some concern about her disappearing, but she hadn't really expected this reaction.

"But I've come back with a gift," Sage said, lifting the small package. She placed it carefully on the table before him and watched for any reaction.

"It's a tonic," she said, her voice no more than a whisper. "It will heal you; I think."

Prince Finn smiled and reached out to take the package. He opened it carefully and looked inside. His eyes widened as he saw the glass vial that held the deep golden tonic. He looked up at Sage, a question in his gaze.

"It's made from specific bees with particular plants and processed by *only* other fire mages," she explained. "It's a long shot, and I doubt it will heal you right away, but I have ideas of ways to improve it over time. I hope it works."

Prince Finn's eyes beamed with hope. He reached out to take her hands and gently squeezed them.

"Thank you, honeybee," he said, his voice sincere.

Sage smiled and looked away, emotion flooding through her. He was arrogant and condescending, yet the more she thought about the little moments they had shared together alone, he was also thoughtful and sincere. Why did he make her feel this way?

"You're welcome," she said.

Prince Finn looked down at the package in his hands, then back at Sage. He held her gaze, and she returned it, her heart suddenly filling with warmth.

"I will try it. Any idea what to expect?" his voice filled with determination.

She offered him a small grin. "Not in the slightest."

He looked at the bottle, then took a deep breath and drank it in one long gulp as if he were afraid that someone might snatch it away.

When the vial was empty, Sage took it from him and set it on the table. Her eyes searched his face.

"How was it?"

"It was a strange sensation, like a million tiny needles pricking my throat as the tonic slid down. But it was also strangely calming."

"Do you feel different?" she asked.

Prince Finn nodded, his eyes locked with hers.

"Yes. A little."

"May I check?" she asked.

Sage reached out hesitantly and, after a slight nod of agreement from him, touched Prince Finn's hands. The warmth of his skin seeped into her palm, and a shiver ran through her body. She tried to focus on what she was doing rather than be distracted by how his hands felt and examined them carefully. His nails had been an unhealthy grey before, but now they were slowly beginning to regain their natural color.

"I think it's working," she whispered in awe as she traced a finger over his hand.

Prince Finn smiled at her, a look of relief washing over him. "Thank you for your help."

Sage was caught in his gaze before looking away embarrassed. She cleared her throat and distanced herself from him, trying to compose herself.

"You're welcome," she said, voice barely above a whisper.

Prince Finn nodded and turned his attention back to the vial on the table, lifting it to look at it more closely.

"How many more times will I need to do this?" he asked thoughtfully.

"I'm unsure. If you could tell me more about your magic, I may be able to create a more potent dose. It takes time to create and requires the help of others, but I am hopeful. While I only see a small change, it is still an improvement."

The two sat silently before Sage adjusted on her pillow, breaking the comfortable stillness between them.

"I should inform Rachel of the results. I will need her help along with Nectars Embrace to create more of this," she said gesturing toward the door with her head, indicating that it was time for her to leave.

Prince Finn's eyes widened.

"You found Nectars Embrace? They are practically a legend."

Sage laughed a little. "Apparently, they are much more active and involved in your kingdom than you realize. It's who I brought with me. I would never have found them if I hadn't gone to help Rosey."

"Will you need to return there?" he asked hesitantly.

Sage hoped he was asking because he didn't want her to leave again, but she couldn't think like that. She nodded.

"Possibly. I may be able to work something out with them where we can send information and vials back and forth, but I may need to be more hands-on as well."

Prince Finn sighed and ran a hand through his hair, frustration apparent on his face. He seemed conflicted and was obviously worried about her going back, but he managed to compose himself enough to give her a tight smile.

"Don't worry," she said, leaning across the table and lightly touching his arm. "I'm not giving up on helping you."

Prince Finn looked down at where her hand rested. He cleared his throat as if trying to shake off the feeling.

"I understand." He nodded as Sage removed her hand and leaned back onto her cushion. "Let me know when you need help. What do you need to know about my magic?"

Everhunt

S age left Prince Finn's tent, and to her surprise, the sun had already set. Their conversation had left her with a jumble of thoughts and feelings. He had seemed so alone and yet so full of passion. Notes of everything she could think to ask about his fire magic were now tucked safely in her pocket, along with her ideas to share with Rachel when she saw her next.

As Sage returned to the large tent, she was drawn to the sound of laughter coming from inside. She looked in to find Asher, Sawyer, and Colby seated around a table, playing a card game.

Sawyer spotted her and waved. "Sage! Are you going to join us? We're just playing Everhunt and could use a fourth."

"I don't know how to play." she admitted. Their cards showed detailed illustrations of dragons and other fantastical creatures.

"It's easy. We can teach you," Asher said, gathering the cards. "Okay, the basic rules are—"

"No, no, no," Sawyer interjected. "That's not how it works. You need to tell her the point of the game first! The rules don't make much sense without knowing why you must follow them."

Colby rolled his eyes. "Just let him explain. Then we can get into the goals of the game."

"Right," Asher continued. "So as I was saying, Everhunt is a card game where two or more players attempt to build the strongest dragon and ultimately have the largest hoard at the end of the game. The object is to power up your dragon and win items that add to your hoard. The person with the largest hoard at the end of the game wins."

"But," Sawyer jumped in again, "if you don't strategize your moves carefully, you can find yourself in a tough spot."

"That's right." Colby nodded. " It's an intense game, and you gotta be smart if you wanna win."

Sage listened intently as Asher, Sawyer, and Colby continued explaining different strategies for playing and how each item worked as she examined some of their cards. She wasn't sure if she understood it all, but it looked like a lot of fun.

When Asher concluded his explanation, he glanced at her face to gauge her understanding. Satisfied, he closed his mouth and clapped his hands together. Placing his hands on the tabletop, he shuffled the card decks with practiced ease before dealing out four hands of eight cards and placing the rest aside.

"Okay," Asher began as everyone picked up their cards, "now let's start. Everyone pick one card from your hand and place it face down before you."

Sage followed Asher's instructions and chose a card. She placed it face down on the table, feeling a bit nervous. What if she chose something totally useless?

"Now," Asher continued, "place the rest of your cards on your right face down for the person beside you to use. Before you pick up your new deck, flip over the one you selected to keep."

One by one, they did as instructed.

Sage looked around the table at the face-up cards and found that each had chosen a dragon that matched their natural magical ability. Her laugh earned her raised brows, but she said nothing.

Sage gulped before turning over her fire dragon card, and she honestly didn't know what to choose to help it. What could she choose that would make a strong dragon?

After arranging the cards she got from Asher in her hand, she drew another card to get her hand back to eight and studied them for what felt like forever. Sage finally selected a spell card and added it to the table upside down before pushing the remaining ones beside her to Colby. He took them eagerly, his eyes lighting up as he examined them with interest.

Some items only worked for certain types of dragons, and others took multiples to earn any points. It wasn't until everyone started playing that Sage understood what was going on—how some items worked better together than others or how some strategies led to more significant rewards. In contrast, others cost you points at the end of the game.

The game moved quickly as each player maneuvered their way around their opponents, trying to power up their dragon and amass the biggest hoard possible by trading off items or earning bonuses from their luckiest draws.

As soon as the attacks began, the air was rife with tension. Bets were raised, and Asher thrust his earth dragon into the fray.

"Time to get greedy!" he cackled.

Sage was caught off guard but not for long. "Well, if that's how you want to play it," she grinned, flipping over two defense cards and launching a retaliatory strike. "Let's see how much loot I can get away with!"

After a few moments of intense concentration, Sage managed to overpower Asher's attack and claimed three pieces of loot. With her newfound bounty, she began building up her dragon even further by adding artifacts and spells that would grant it increased power in future battles.

With every card draw, trade-off, or attack made by one player, someone else would counter-attack or try to steal back their lost loot. This cycle continued until Colby had built up an unassailable hoard and was finally declared the winner.

Though disappointed by her loss, Sage was still happy with the results. After all, she hadn't expected to make it this far, given her lack of experience compared to everyone else at the table.

Asher congratulated Colby before turning to Sage with a smile. "You did really well for your first time playing. You held your own and didn't give up even when it seemed hopeless. I'm impressed."

Sage beamed. "Thanks. It was really fun!"

"Glad to have you back," Sawyer said, a large grin spreading across his face as he patted her on the back.

"You were missed," Colby added.

"On that note," Asher winked, "we should find you somewhere to sleep. If you promise not to run off on me again, I may have a place you can stay."

***

Sage woke with a start, unsure of where she was or how she had gotten there. Her eyes darted around the strange room, taking in the unfamiliar furnishings.

She sat there, trying to piece together the previous night's events. She was with the Charming Four and had slept in a side room of Asher's tent. She had started treatment on Prince Finn. A treatment that appeared to be working.

With a groan, she stretched fully on the makeshift bed. Voices quietly carried through the thin tent walls.

Curious, she got out of bed, slipped her dress over her head, and ran her fingers through her hair before opening the flap to join the men.

They sat around a table, talking earnestly. On the table was a folded letter that all four seemed to be discussing. Sage couldn't make out the conversation, but it was clear that their words held an urgency.

Curiosity getting the better of her, Sage stepped forward, but before she could ask what was happening, the four mages suddenly fell silent and turned to her.

"Ah, Sage," Sawyer said, a smile on his face. "Good morning. Sleep well?"

Covering her mouth as a yawn escaped, she nodded yes.

"What's that?" Sage asked, her eyes darting to the letter.

"We have a new mission," Colby answered, practically bouncing in his chair.

"With things beginning to settle down here, I can hand over the repairs and recovery to our military to organize," Prince Finn replied. "We must leave soon."

"So what does that mean for me?" Sage asked, pulling up a chair to join the others at the table.

"You're coming with us," Asher replied.

She couldn't keep the grin from her face. "I am?"

"You are, but," Prince Finn's face was earnest, "you have to stay with us and do what we ask when we ask. You can't run off, or we can't protect you."

She wanted to tell them they didn't need to worry about that. It wasn't something she would do until she realized she had done just that to them. She offered a sheepish grin. "What's the mission? Where are we heading?"

"I'm afraid we can't tell you the details of the mission itself. Not yet, at least, but it may become dangerous. Hopefully, your skills won't be needed, but I wouldn't be surprised if they are," Prince Finn said

Sage nodded and smiled. "Don't worry about me. I won't run off on my own."

Prince Finn's face softened. "I appreciate your assurance, but this mission is dangerous. We shall need all the help we can get."

"It will take us a couple of days to reach where we need to investigate in the mountains," Asher added.

"We must plan our supplies and route carefully," Sawyer said. He began to lay out maps and papers filled with notes on the table before them.

The four mages plunged into planning their journey, and Sage watched the process with keen interest. The group was remarkably efficient, and she could now understand why they weren't a larger guild. Each of them had their role, and as powerful as she knew them all to be, they didn't need anyone else.

As she shook her head at their level of organization, Prince Finn caught her eye from across the room and raised an eyebrow.

Sage thought it over before finally giving a slight nod of agreement as if to say she was ready for whatever this mission entailed. Prince Finn smiled before turning his attention back to his companions, though Sage could feel his approval radiating like a warm hug.

Excusing herself, Sage left the tent because she had things to take care of before they went on their mission.

Making her way across the camp, she found Rachel, who was finishing up her work in the infirmary tent.

"It appears they are keeping you busy," Sage said.

Rachel smiled brightly, her eyes twinkling with joy. "It's my favorite way to live."

"Have you had any luck figuring out what is spreading through the camp?"

"I think so. It appears to be several things, but all are easily treatable. How about you? How has your patient taken to your treatment?"

"It seems to have helped. I only noticed a small change, but it's given me some hope," Sage replied, pulling her notes from her discussion with Prince Finn about his magic from her pocket. "I'm leaving on a mission with the Charming Four soon, and I was hoping that you could help me make some more of the treatment. Of course, I would pay you for your time as well as anyone who is assisting. I asked about their fire magic so we could try and find close matches."

Rachel took the paper and tucked it away. "Of course. I don't mind helping. When do you leave?"

"I don't know yet. They are planning it now. I get the impression that it is soon, though."

"I understand. If you need to restock anything, feel free to do it here. Supplies from Nectars Embrace just arrived this morning. I will just bill it to the Charming Four," Rachel said with a wink.

"Thank you so much," Sage said as she gave Rachel's shoulder an appreciative squeeze.

"It's my pleasure. Now go get ready and good luck on your mission."

Sage gave Rachel a grateful smile before turning away to gather her supplies. No matter how hard she tried, she couldn't shake the feeling of inadequacy that weighed on her shoulders. She tried to push down her envy for the Charming Four and their magical abilities, but it was hard. She wanted to be useful, too. No, she was determined to be useful.

***

Sage stood at the island's edge, her feet planted firmly in the sand, her heart beating a frantic staccato in her chest. She stared ahead at the vista before her, her breath coming in short, shallow gasps. There, between the clouds and the sky, a rope bridge stretched out before her, leading to the island beyond.

Growing up in the capital, Vishneel, meant she had never seen the island's edge before. It was the largest out of the floating kingdom and took days to travel from one edge to the other. She'd never had any reason to leave before.

She felt a warmth on her shoulder and turned to see Prince Finn beside her with a reassuring smile.

"Courage comes in many forms," he said, his voice soothing. "You need only to take the first step."

Sage hesitated, her heart still pounding. She peered across the bridge, seeing that Asher, Colby, and Sawyer were already on their way, their forms silhouetted against the deep blue sky.

"We'll stay the night in the town on the other side," Asher called out to her. "You just have to get there."

"A warm bed and bath are waiting for you over there," Sawyer added.

"Maybe even your own room this time if we get there fast enough!" Colby shouted over his shoulder.

Sage peeked at Prince Finn over her shoulder, remembering what it felt like sleeping next to him. Feeling her cheeks flush, she hid her face and focused on the challenge ahead. Never before had she been afraid of heights. But, at the same time, she had never faced dropping into the vast nothingness below Sarash either.

Steadying her nerves, she stepped onto the bridge's first plank. Her feet felt the rope sway beneath her as she took her small step, her hands outstretched in search of the thin ropes that lined either side of the bridge.

She reached the center, where the wind whipped around, tossing her hair and tugging at her clothes. Looking out at the open sky, she felt a sense of fear and exhilaration.

Her feet slipped out from beneath her, the wind suddenly knocking her off balance. She grasped at the rope, her breaths coming in short shallow gasps as she tried to steady herself. Just as she thought she would fall into the void below, a strong arm encircled her waist, pulling her back to safety.

She gasped and turned to see Prince Finn's face just inches from hers. His dark eyes were intense, and his lips were set in a determined line as he held onto the rope with one hand and kept a secure grip on Sage with the other.

For a moment, they stayed like that, their faces close enough that Sage could feel his breath on her skin. His gaze softened, and he smiled down at her reassuringly. "I've got you, honeybee. I won't let you fall."

Something stirred inside her, and she returned his smile, feeling suddenly safe despite being suspended above the abyss. She stared into Prince Finn's eyes, and for a split second, it was like all her worries had melted into nothingness, and it was just them—alone in eternity together on this bridge between two worlds.

"Thank you," she whispered, her voice barely audible over the wind.

Prince Finn smiled and nodded, then released his grip on her waist. He stepped back and gestured for her to continue. Sage looked at him before turning back toward the end of the bridge.

The Hot Spring

A s promised, Sage had a room to herself at the hot springs on the new island. It was beautiful, with a large bed that had the softest sheets she had ever felt and a balcony with an incredible view of the sea of clouds between the two islands. While she wasn't a fan of the crossing, she could appreciate the view's beauty from afar.

Before joining the others for dinner, Sage decided to dip in the hot spring. Something to help her relax after a long day of hiking.

Sage followed the winding stone path until she arrived at the entrance. She paused in awe of the building, with intricate architecture, marble pillars, and tall statues. Three doors sat near each other on one wall. One for men, one for women, and the last where both were welcome.

She hesitated before pushing the woman's door open, unsure what to find inside. The room was small and steamy, with a few rough-hewn wooden benches scattered around the edges. A handful of women were lounging on them, chatting in low voices. In the center of the room was a shallow pool filled with bubbling hot water. As she approached, she saw several more women soaking in it, their bodies glistening with moisture.

She chose one of the empty dressing rooms and stripped off her clothes, feeling awkward and exposed. Her hands shook when she emerged, naked as everyone else. It was as if all the conventions of clothing and modesty had been stripped away along with her garments.

The steamy waters were inviting, and Sage quickly found a spot. She sank into the pool, the warm waters soothing her muscles and the steamy air filling her lungs. For the first time in days, she felt at ease. The world seemed to drift away as she sank deeper until the sound of male voices caught her attention.

The muffled voices belonged to Prince Finn, Asher, Sawyer, and Colby. Something about dragons and a mission. Intrigued, Sage leaned closer to the wall to try and make out the rest of the conversation.

"The report said there were signs in the mountains near Hartshire," Prince Finn said.

"How reliable is the report?" Asher piped up.

"As good as any we are going to get for this," Sawyer said.

"Then it's settled," Colby said. "We'll head there in the morning."

"Do you think she will make it?" Sawyer asked. "It's going to be rough, and she hasn't been training for these sorts of missions like we have."

Asher's voice was extra quiet, and Sage had to strain to hear as many of the words he was saying as she could: "She should be fine."

"If we need to, we can always call Finn for help. He will save her." She heard a splash and the men laughing. "We all saw you two on the bridge," Colby said. "When did that start?"

"I don't know what you're talking about," Prince Finn said. She could almost hear the smile in his voice.

A group of women moved nearby, their voices drowning out the Charming Four's discussion.

Sage's heart fluttered. Alone without other responsibilities, she allowed her mind to wander to Prince Finn. His behavior had grown more attentive and kind toward her as of late. Perhaps hers had in return. Had she developed feelings for him?

She strained to listen, but it was impossible. They were talking about her, right? Sage sank further into the pool in an attempt to hide her embarrassment. That didn't make any sense. Prince Finn would never be interested in someone like her. She wasn't noble; she was average in every way. She shook her head. Why was she worrying about this anyway? Did she want him to find her as more?

With a contented sigh, Sage sank up to her neck into the warm waters of the hot springs and allowed herself to drift off with thoughts of the future. After completely losing track of time, she was brought back to the present by her stomach's grumble. Not yet ready to leave the warm water, even though her body resembled a prune, she reluctantly pulled herself out and wrapped her body in a fresh linen robe from a cart near the dressing room entrance.

After gathering her belongings and remaining barefoot, instead of attempting to slip her wet feet into her boots, she exited the women's dressing room and headed to her room. Her feet hit a wet spot on the stone floor, and her eyes flew open as she slipped, releasing a sharp gasp of pain and fear. Trying to catch herself, she stumbled back, her head hitting the stone wall, and tumbled onto the ground.

Sage tried to stand but found her legs wouldn't hold her weight, her vision blurring as a wave of dizziness passed over her.

Strong arms caught her before she could hit the ground, placing her in a sitting position. Through the fog of confusion, Sage realized that Prince Finn had caught her. He gently brushed some stray hairs away from her face. "Are you alright?"

Sage nodded weakly, though inside, she felt anything but alright. She gingerly touched the spot where she had hit her head, feeling wetness on her fingertips when she pulled them away. Her breath quickened as panic set in, realizing that she was bleeding.

"Easy," Prince Finn said in a soothing voice as he used his free hand to brush away tears that had started streaming down Sage's face. She looked up at him, so close now yet still so far away—his royal status separating them like an impenetrable wall between two worlds.

Prince Finn picked up a cloth from the pile he had dropped to catch her. He held it against Sage's wound to stop the bleeding before helping her back to her room so they could clean and bandage it properly.

Once they were done with their ministrations, Prince Finn gave Sage one last concerned look before standing up from kneeling next to her. "I think you should stay here tonight. I can bring you food."

Sage stared at him in surprise. Was he really doing this for her? Taking care of someone else. It somehow seemed very un-princely and unlike how she had always imagined princes were. A warmth filled Sage's chest. It was like her worries and fears were melting away, and she felt safe.

"Thank you," she whispered.

Prince Finn gave her a small smile before leaving the room, so Sage could be alone with her thoughts.

Head throbbing, Sage slipped in and out of consciousness. At one point, she became aware that she was still only wearing a robe, and embarrassment flooded her cheeks. She thought of Prince Finn, hoping he hadn't noticed her state of undress, or at the very least, hadn't seen too much.

Sage tried to stand, wanting to get properly dressed in her overshirt before he returned. But as soon as she put weight on her feet, they shook beneath her and her head swam. The entire room seemed to be moving around her as though her body were in molasses. With a gasp, she fell back, and to her surprise, Prince Finn caught her before she could hit the ground and helped her onto the mattress.

"It's alright," he said, placing a reassuring hand on Sage's shoulder. "What do you need?"

"I want to get dressed," she mumbled, embarrassed to be so helpless. A feeling she hated.

He glanced at her pack at the foot of the bed. "What do you want to change into?"

"My shirt. I just want to sleep in my shirt."

"Let me help you," Prince Finn offered, sitting on the bed next to Sage and slipping his shirt over his head. "It's clean and will cover you better than yours. Until you are better, it's best to have one of us with you."

Sage's heart raced as she tried not to stare at his bare chest. Of course, he was right. She may need help during the night, and his shirt would cover more than hers.

He helped her face away from him with gentle hands and eased off Sage's shirt before replacing it with his. As his fingers brushed against hers, she leaned into him ever so slightly.

Prince Finn didn't seem to notice as he helped her slip back under the blanket—or perhaps he just chose not to comment on it—instead continuing to talk in soothing tones until finally he was done. His words faded in and out as she breathed in his scent from his shirt. She snuggled deeper into her bed, afraid to admit even to herself how much she was enjoying his attention and how afraid she was that she was overthinking everything.

Prince Finn pulled away as soon as he heard voices in the hall. Asher, Sawyer, and Colby burst into the room with concerned looks.

Sage blushed at being caught in such an intimate moment, but she was glad to see them and the food they carried. They would take care of her.

"So, what's going on here?" Asher asked jokingly, taking in the sight of Prince Finn topless.

"Just helping her get dressed," Prince Finn said, completely avoiding the state of his undress.

"Yeah, I can see that." Colby smirked before turning to Sage. "How are you feeling?"

Sage nodded slowly, not wanting to appear weak. She was tempted to lie and say she would be fine by tomorrow, but she remembered their conversation in the hot spring. Already they were worried she wouldn't be able to handle traveling in the mountains. Attempting to do so while injured wouldn't help anyone.

"I've been better," she admitted.

Prince Finn grabbed the food Sawyer was carrying and placed it on the nightstand next to Sage. "Someone should stay here with Sage while the rest scout ahead tomorrow," he said, before pausing. "We will wait to act on anything found until we can all go together." His voice was firm and confident despite the seriousness of the situation.

Sawyer, Asher, and Colby nodded at Prince Finn's suggestion. A wave of relief washed over her at knowing she wouldn't be alone. She was grateful for the prince's concern. Although it was strange to think someone would stay behind just for her.

The group stayed in her room chatting and joking around until late at night. The conversation between Asher and Sawyer always turned into an argument about who was better at what—whether it was hunting or cooking—until finally, Colby had to intervene and settle the score.

Prince Finn remained quiet throughout most of their banter but offered a few witty remarks here and there when needed, making them all laugh.

Sage found herself wishing that this moment would never end. Despite her exhaustion, she wanted to stay here with them forever.

Her eyes grew heavier and heavier as the night drew on, and eventually, she was left with only Asher in her room to help if she needed anything.

As she drifted off to sleep, Sage couldn't help but feel safe with these four men, like nothing bad could ever happen so long as they were together.

***

Sawyer and Sage sat on the hot spring's balcony, the warm smell of minerals wafting up from the steamy waters. Sage got up, leaned against the balcony rail, and gazed out at the puffy clouds below.

The two had been sitting there in companionable silence, each lost in their thoughts for most of the day. The rest of the Charming Four had left earlier that morning and weren't expected back for a few more hours. Sage was grateful to have someone to share the moment with, to listen to the breeze and the birds' songs in the trees. But then, something caught their eye.

Sawyer and Sage watched with interest, focusing on the group of people crossing the rope bridge below. There were five of them, and in the center was a tall figure, broad of shoulder, and wearing a hooded cloak. Sage frowned at the sight of him; she knew who it was.

"That's the crown prince," she said, her voice low. "What is he doing here and under disguise?"

Sawyer clenched his fists. "It can't be good. We still haven't figured out why he had you make that potion for him."

"Has he done anything out of the ordinary?"

"No. Nothing."

The group neared the island's edge. "And now he's here," Sage said, "finally doing something unusual. I'm sure he has something planned."

Sawyer nodded. "I need to see what he's up to. Stay here."

Sage sighed. "Sawyer, you're not going without me. You guys made me promise to stay near one of you on this trip at all times."

"We also said you had to listen to our orders if we gave them. Sage, you are injured. If you come with me, you will be more of a hindrance than a help. I'm not going to engage with them. Only scout."

Sage crossed her arms and frowned. "I won't be in your way."

"This is no time for arguing," Sawyer said, his voice firm. "Stay here." He turned to go but stopped when he felt Sage's hand on his arm. He looked down and saw the concern in her eyes.

"Be careful," she said before letting him go. He gave her a small smile before slipping quietly through the trees, heading toward the group.

The crown prince and his group reached the island, and, from the balcony, Sage stiffened when she saw Sawyer creeping too close. A guard yelled out when Sawyer was spotted, and she wanted to cry out as they attacked him.

He threw up walls of ice, separating him and his attackers, as he looked for a way to escape. Sage wrapped her arms around herself as the guards broke through Sawyer's ice walls and attacked him.

An idea struck her. She grabbed her pack and hobbled down the stairs toward Sawyer and his attackers as fast as her injured body would let her.

She made it to the street where Sawyer was fighting off his attackers with ice spears. They outnumbered him, and Sage feared he wouldn't be able to fight them all off by himself. Taking a deep breath, she steeled herself for what she was about to do and pulled two bottles from her bag. She smashed them on the ground beside each other and a heavy purple fog multiplied and rolled toward the Crown Prince and his men.

The guards were momentarily stunned by this sudden attack, giving Sawyer enough time to escape into the nearby trees.

Sage breathed a sigh of relief and turned around—only to find herself face-to-face with the crown prince.

The prince smirked, delighting in his victory. "I see we meet again. It appears you are working for my brother in more ways than I originally expected," he said sinisterly, clamping down on her arm and tugging her along after him. His guards followed close behind.

Sage tried to pull her arm free from the prince's grip, but he held tight, his fingers digging into her skin. She gritted her teeth and followed him, her heart pounding. She had to stay calm and figure out a way to escape from him and his guards.

"What do you want from me, Your Highness?" she asked, steadying her voice.

"Oh, nothing much." His eyes gleamed with amusement. "Just a little chat. I'm sure you have some interesting stories about my dear brother's activities. I promise no harm will come to you if you listen and do what we say."

Sage shook her head as her mind worked out how he could have twisted his words. Fae may not be able to lie, but they were the best at working loopholes into their speech. "I don't know what you're talking about. I'm just a librarian and an apothecary. I don't involve myself in politics."

The crown prince laughed. "Don't insult my intelligence, Sage. I know you are on a mission for my brother and his group, looking for something. Something powerful. And I want to know where it is."

Sage swallowed hard as she tried to come up with a plan. She couldn't give away any information, even if she had it. The crown prince was dangerous and she didn't know what he would do if he found what he was looking for.

"I don't know what you're talking about," she repeated, her tone firm.

The prince's grip on her arm tightened, and Sage winced. "I don't believe you," he said, his eyes narrowing. "But that's alright. We'll find out one way or another."

One of the prince's guards bound Sage's hands with rope and led her by the arm. The other guards remained close behind them as they made their way through the small town and out onto a dirt path that led into the forest.

Sage glanced around, hoping to catch sight of Sawyer following from a distance. But she saw no sign of him, and her heart sank. She felt so helpless and alone, not knowing what to do but follow her captors.

The group marched on in silence until they reached the foothills of a large mountain range. Sage gasped when she saw it—its size and beauty were magnificent and awe-inspiring. But fear replaced wonder as they ascended the steep path that wound its way up the mountain side. Her vision was starting to darken and she was afraid her legs would not carry her much further. What would they do if she suddenly collapsed? Leave her? Worse?

She looked desperately around for something to help her escape, but there was nothing except tree after tree, stretching high into the sky. Her only hope now was to wait for an opportunity to present itself—something that would enable her to get away before it was too late.

Sage clung to a thin thread of hope as she trudged along the winding path, her captors dragging her along. The guards and crown prince were on alert and silent, leaving Sage with nothing but her thoughts for company.

At last, they stopped to set up camp for the night. Sage was relieved when they untied her hands so she could sit near the fire they had started. The crown prince reached into his pocket and pulled out the bottle of fake poison she had given him.

"I'm sure you remember this. I never expected that you would get to see the results firsthand." He still didn't know it was fake, and a surge of fear coursed through her veins as he held it up to the fading light.

Sage's heart pounded as the crown prince examine the bottle of fake poison. He would be furious when he found out it wasn't real. She had to think of something quickly to keep up the façade.

"I do remember it," she said, her voice shaking slightly. "I hope you found it to be effective."

The crown prince smirked. "We will find out soon. Are you sure you don't know what my brother and his friends are up to?"

Sage tried to keep her expression neutral, but inside, she was relieved. At least her deception had worked for the moment, and he had yet to mention the state she had left him when she slipped the mad honey into his tea. But she couldn't keep up the lie forever. Eventually, he would discover the truth, and then she would be in even more danger.

The crown prince looked at Sage expectantly, waiting for her to say something. She tried to think of an answer to appease him without revealing too much.

"I'm sorry, I was not told about the mission. I was brought along only for medical purposes," she said carefully.

He scowled but seemed to accept her answer. "Very well. Would you like to know my guess?" He paused, his eyes locked with hers. "There have been rumors of dragon sightings in these mountains," he said, watching her reaction. "Could it be possible that Prince Finn was also here looking for dragons?" The crown prince seemed to read the surprise in her eyes as fear and smiled knowingly. "It appears we are both after the same prize," he said smugly.

Sage swallowed hard, knowing she had no choice but to continue the charade. She nodded slowly and forced a small smile, even though she felt anything but happy.

The crown prince reached into his pocket and pulled out the fake poison bottle he had been clutching earlier. He held it up so that it gleamed in the firelight, making Sage shudder at the thought of what horrors it could bring if she had made it correctly.

"We'll use this on them," he stated bluntly, finally revealing his plans with a wicked grin.

Among Dragons

T he day had been long as the crown prince and his guards led Sage deeper into the mountains. The steep paths with cliffs running on either side were even more treacherous, with her hands tied in front, unable to assist if she made a wrong step.

As they continued their journey, Sage's thoughts shifted from the view to the prince. She had only met him a few times, and she found it unsettling that he had taken such an interest in her. Sage could sense he was deep in thought.

"I know you do not like dragons, Your Highness.," she said hesitantly. "But why?" She wanted to know what was on his mind. "What is it about them that frightens you so much?"

The prince huffed and looked at the sky with a heavy expression. "I'm not scared of them. You must remember the war between the fae and dragons many years ago," he said gravely. "The fae were greatly outnumbered and outmatched by their opponents. We almost lost."

He sighed before rubbing along his jaw. "If the dragons ever returned, I fear they would bring destruction and chaos to our lands once more. From what I have heard, they are savage creatures with no regard for life or justice and I do not wish to see my people suffer under their reign again."

Sage nodded slowly. She had never seen a dragon before but knew enough of their destructive power to understand why the crown prince wanted to prevent them from returning. She gazed ahead in thought.

"Your Highness, I understand but may I suggest something? Perhaps if we learn more about these creatures, we can better prepare ourselves for future encounters with them. Knowledge about our enemy can be just as powerful as any weapon we possess against them."

"It's not that simple. The fae made that mistake once before, and we will not do it again."

"What do you mean?"

"Do you know what started the war?"

Sage shook her head no, only to remember that he was walking before her and couldn't see her response. "No."

"There was a peace treaty between the fae and dragons. Our islands were split. Dragons killed several fae, which broke the treaty."

Sage was still curious. "Do you know why the dragons killed the fae? What happened?"

The crown prince shook his head. "No one knows for certain. It could have been revenge or a dispute over territory—It doesn't matter now. All I know is that I cannot risk my people being harmed again if there is a chance that the dragons may return."

Sage frowned thoughtfully. It was clear that the prince's experience had left behind a deep-seated loathing of these creatures. "Your Highness," she spoke softly, her words full of compassion, "hatred breeds hatred, and violence begets only more violence. We should not judge an entire race from their past sins. They may have changed, and we should be open to discovering more about them before we pass judgment."

Prince Owen stared back at her before finally nodding. He seemed pensive, like he was mulling over something. He rubbed the back of his neck and looked up at the mountain wall beside them.

"You are right, Sage," he said after a while, determination in his voice. "I cannot judge an entire species based on the actions of a few. But I cannot deny the potential for the destruction they can bring."

Sage admired his courage to defend his people, but she also pitied him for his hatred of the dragons. To her, they were majestic creatures, symbols of strength and power

The sky suddenly grew dark as the procession rounded a sharp corner. Sage blinked, unable to make out what was ahead. The prince had stopped, and his guards were murmuring among themselves. As her eyes adjusted to the darkness, Sage realized they had reached the mouth of a cave.

Prince Owen grasped the rope attached to Sage's wrists. "This is our destination." His voice rose above the wind as he pointed into the darkness. "If they are in these mountains, this is where we will find them."

A chill ran down her spine. In the cave, she could not see the prince's face, but she could tell he was not afraid—he was ready to face whatever danger lurked beyond. Sage followed him inside, her heart pounding with anticipation.

The rest of the group ventured after them, guided only by the faint glimmer of fire in the crown prince's outstretched hands. The further they traveled, the darker and colder it became until, finally, it seemed as if they had reached an impenetrable wall of blackness.

Prince Owen stopped and held his flames aloft. Sage could make out a large opening in the darkness ahead—the entrance to what appeared to be a vast underground chamber. She shivered, cursing her- self for not having grabbed her cloak before trying to help Sawyer. At least she felt stronger since injur- ing herself yesterday.

But then, Sage remembered why they were there and turned to Prince Owen. "Your Highness," she asked in a small voice, "what is your plan for get- ting that potion into the dragon's mouth? And what will you do if there's more than one? That won't be enough to take care of multiple dragons."

The prince smiled grimly at her question before stepping into the chamber, his flames lighting up his face beneath his mask. "My plan is simple: I will use my fire magic to lure them out of their lair one by one," he said confidently. "And with Treston here," he pointed to one of the guards behind her, "using his glamour magic, we can create more bottles and return as many times as necessary. Being one of the most powerful glamour mages they should stick around long enough to get the job done before disappearing. Jackson," he pointed to another one of his guards, "will keep them asleep as we work. The others are here as my backup plan if this all goes sideways. No need for you to know any of that, though."

Sage nodded while her heart beat rapidly as she thought of all that could go wrong. But she put her fears aside and diligently followed him into the chamber's depths. They soon encountered several sleeping dragons within its confines, their scales shimmering like moonlight whenever the crown prince's firelight hit them.

Sage gazed at the six giant dragons. They were more magnificent than she had dared to imagine. Despite her fear of them, admiration coursed through her for these beautiful creatures.

Sage noticed several large eggs tucked partially beneath two of the dragons. Her heart sank as she realized what this meant—even though her potion wouldn't kill the giant dragons, she had no way of knowing what effect it would have on them. What would the crowned prince do to them?

She stepped closer to get a better look and noticed that one of the eggs had started to crack open. She gasped in surprise and quickly backed away, hoping none of the dragons had noticed her presence.

Sage followed Treston as he slowly advanced, his glamour magic ready to create more bottles. Prince Owen carefully positioned himself near each dragon's mouth while Treston used his magic to create bottle after bottle. Before long, all of them were filled with potions and ready for delivery. Jackson stood guard behind them, prepared to put any dragon that awoke back into its slumber.

Sage kept her distance as the five men worked to pour the potion into each dragon's mouth. She felt helpless, powerless to do anything but watch. She was relieved to know that her potion shouldn't kill the dragons but was afraid the prince would forfeit her life once he discovered the truth. What would happen when he found out his potion had not worked as intended? What would he do to her then?

As she searched for a way to escape, she noticed a small alcove near the back of the chamber. It was far enough away from where they were working that she could slip away without being noticed. She rushed over, her heart pounding.

Once Sage was safely tucked away, she waited anxiously for the potion's effects to take hold. After what seemed like an eternity, a roar echoed through the chamber as each dragon awoke, angry.

Prince Owen and his men acted quickly; Jackson used his spellcasting to attempt to put each dragon back into a deep sleep while Treston created more potion bottles. Sage watched with bated breath as they worked, hoping their plan would fail and she could find a way to escape.

Sage huddled with dread in her hiding place, the loud roars of the dragons echoing through the chamber. Flames erupted from their mouths, lighting up the room as they tried to attack the fae men. With their magic, the fae held their own against the dragons, but each spell seemed to stun the dragons momentarily instead of subduing them.

One of the dragons lunged forward and grabbed one of the guards in its mouth. Sage gasped in horror as it made its way toward a tunnel at the back of the chamber. She was about to scream when she realized that any noise would give away her hiding place.

With a sinking feeling in her stomach, Sage watched as Prince Owen and his men slowly lost their fight against the dragons. They were running out of options, and soon it seemed like it was only a matter of time before the dragons defeated them. As if sensing her thoughts, one of the dragons turned toward her hiding spot and began approaching.

She stumbled backward, panic coursing through her veins as she frantically searched for somewhere else to hide or an escape route. Just when she thought all hope was lost, Prince Owen noticed what was happening and used his magic to distract the dragon. He shouted for Sage to make a run for it while he held off the beast.

Sage didn't hesitate; she bolted from her hiding spot and raced for one of the tunnels on the other side of the chamber. The one they had entered from was blocked by the fight, but perhaps the one the dragon had taken the guard down could help her escape if she didn't get eaten first. She could hear claws scraping against the stone behind her as she ran, but thankfully it seemed like whatever spell the prince had cast had slowed the dragon.

Sage darted toward the tunnel, her heart pounding with adrenalin. She was almost there when she noticed something out of the corner of her eye—Prince Owen fighting with one of the dragons that had been protecting three eggs. The dragon roared back in response to the attack, almost stepping on the eggs. Sage changed course and ran toward them, covering them with her body while rolling them away from danger.

The eggs cracked as they tumbled, and a little dragon's head popped out, looking at Sage with wide eyes. Knowing they were safe for now, Sage scrambled back to her feet and headed for the tunnel again.

She hesitated before diving into the tunnel's darkness, not sure if she would make it safely back out alive. Her hands grazed the dark tunnel's walls, her heart pounding and her breath becoming heavier.

The clicking claws only made her move faster. She stumbled over her feet several times before regaining her balance.

As she continued through the tunnel, something soft nuzzled against her leg. Startled by this unexpected contact, she jumped, nearly screaming until she realized it was a dragonling that had followed her. Its small eyes glowed a dim gold in the dark.

Her heart warmed at the little creature now curling itself around her leg. She should return the dragonling but wasn't sure how the other dragons would take it. While considering what to do, Sage realized she had made a major mistake. In the dark, she had taken her hand off the wall and had moved around with the dragonling so she no longer knew which direction led to the dragons. Her hand ran down the scaled back of the dragonling before she stood, chose a direction, placed her hand on the wall, and began making her way in the dark once again.

Soon a dim light appeared in the distance. When she reached the tunnel's end, all that awaited them was a large opening in the side of a mountain with no obvious way to climb down or escape. Sage stopped, surveying their surroundings in case some hidden path or secret exit existed, but all appeared quiet and empty, with no sign of dragons or fae guarding this entrance, at least not yet anyway.

As she turned to leave, she heard a faint growling. Sage whirled around and the outside light allowed her to see a large dragon with razor-sharp teeth and piercing green eyes. This was not the kind of dragon she was expecting to encounter. Her heart skipped a beat as she realized the creature was blocking her way.

Sage's palms grew sweaty as she tried to back away, and the dragon seemed to be inching closer and closer with every passing second. Its eyes glanced back and forth between her and the dragonling. She had to do something fast before the dragon attacked her. She thought back to all her mother's stories about dragons and how to communicate with them. Taking a deep breath, she slowly extended her hand toward the dragon in a gesture of peace.

The dragon seemed to hesitate before leaning forward and sniffing her hand. Hot breath passed over her fingertips, but instead of biting her, the dragon nuzzled its nose against her palm.

She sighed in relief that she had managed to communicate with the dragon. The dragonling by her side let out a chirping noise, which seemed to attract the attention of the larger dragon. Sage could see the curiosity in the dragon's eyes as it looked at the dragonling.

She slowly reached for the dragonling and held it up toward the larger one. The dragonling sniffed the larger one's nose, and the two seemed to exchange a silent message before the larger dragon let out a deep rumbling purr. Sage couldn't believe her eyes as they nuzzled each other and couldn't help but wonder if this was the parent. It didn't matter, really, as long as the larger one accepted the dragonling and, in turn, accepted Sage as well.

Without thinking, Sage stepped away from the two to give them space, only to find her feet slipping out from under her. She tumbled out of the large entrance to the cave and found herself falling with nothing to grab onto other than the sheer rock cliff, which she knew would injure her if she grabbed it wrong. Her mind raced: What could she do?

Sage's heart raced as she hurtled toward the rocky cliff face, moments away from certain death. She steeled herself for impact when a sudden small sound pierced the air—the screech of a dragonling emerging from above her. Fear coursed through Sage's veins as a giant dragon flew out of the cave and dove with incredible speed toward her. Its talons grasped her and, with one powerful flap of its wings, they were soaring to safety to the bottom of the mountain, where it delicately placed her on solid ground.

As she lay there, an image flashed in her mind; it was of herself saving the dragon eggs from earlier. She could almost feel a sense of thanks from the dragon as if it were trying to communicate with her in some way.

This must be how dragons communicated with each other—through images and feelings rather than words. She smiled as she looked up at the drag-on that was now staring back at her with curiosity. Only a moment passed before the dragonling joined them. Its first flight was unsure and haphazard as it learned to use its wings.

A giggle escaped Sage as it attempted to land, only to find itself in a tangle of its wings on the hard stone floor. The large dragon nuzzled the dragonling, checking for injury before returning its focus to her.

Sage couldn't remember any other ways to communicate with the dragons. They were obviously intelligent, especially if they had been part of a treaty at one point in time.

"Thank you," Sage said. "For saving me, I mean."

She watched the dragons for any sign of understanding. Another image of the dragonling following her into the tunnel flashed in her head.

Sage swallowed, her throat suddenly dry. "I didn't know it was following me. I didn't mean to take it."

More images flashed in her mind. Disappearing as quickly as they appeared. A large silver dragon with a fae on its back. Them eating together in the forest. The fae tossing part of their meal for the dragon to catch. Scene after scene flashed, all accompanied with the sense of friendship and a deep bond.

The large dragon nudged the dragonling toward Sage.

"What do you mean?" she asked.

For a moment nothing happened until one last image appeared in her mind. She startled at the view of her own face. Fire engulfed the dragon behind her and a single feeling was sent to her. The feeling of family. Her heart melted a little as her gaze moved to the dragonling looking up at her. It had claimed her as family.

Found Family

Rocks rained down upon Sage as a figure, who she recognized as the crown prince, scrambled down from the rocky ledge above her. The thunderous roar of an enraged dragon followed close behind him. With a loud yell, he lost his grip and tumbled to the ground in a heap at Sage's feet. Before she could react, the dragon chasing him had also plummeted, and its long tail collided with her body, sending her flying into the rock wall beside her.

The rock wall met her face, the dragon's tail pinned under a rock, as she groaned in pain. The dust around her swirled with the chaos of the dragons chasing the prince, their wings flapping and creating dust clouds. Above the howling of the dragon, Sage heard a voice.

"Sage!" It was Prince Finn, his urgency ringing throughout the canyon. "Get out of the way!"

Sage was pulled to the side. Sawyer, Colby, and Asher surrounded her, their magic ready. The prince's hands firmly gripped her shoulders and a reassuring warmth rushed through her.

"Are you okay?" he asked, assessing her for any injuries.

Sage nodded and then looked back in shock. The large dragon and the dragonling had also followed suit and were now standing guard around Sage and the Charming Four, ready to protect them from further attack. Sage felt a swell of pride and respect toward her newfound guardians and blinked back tears.

Prince Finn turned to Sage, his eyes full of concern. "What's going on?"

He let go of her shoulders and stepped away, moving toward the prone figure of his brother. As the dragons watched him warily, he bent down to see if his brother was still alive. After confirming that he was, Finn straightened and addressed them all.

"I am Prince Finn," he began, his voice strong and determined. "I have been looking for you in order to form a new treaty between our peoples, now that your numbers seem to be growing again enough to be noticed. I would ask you to do me this one favor; let me take my brother with me to be punished by the fae court."

The dragons exchanged looks before one of them stepped forward and images flashed in Sage's mind.

"They accept your offer," she said. "However, they insist that you make sure that your brother is brought to justice in accordance with fae law. They do not approve of rogue behavior such as what they have witnessed today especially if there is any chance of the treaty happening."

The Charming Four looked at her wide-eyed.

"How do you know what they said?" Asher said.

"You didn't see it?" she asked.

They all shook their heads no.

"It's alright. We can figure that out later," Colby added.

Finn nodded solemnly and then knelt to pick up his unconscious brother. He turned to Sage and their friends and held out a hand for assistance. Without hesitation, they each grabbed onto one arm or leg of his brother's body and helped him carry him away.

Sage glanced back at the dragons as they watched them go, their expressions unreadable, but a dragonling trailed her.

"What's happening here?" Sawyer asked.

"I apparently bonded with a dragon. Don't ask me how. I have no idea," Sage answered.

"So, where exactly are we supposed to keep a dragon in the capital?" Colby asked.

Prince Finn grunted as he shifted his grip on his brother. "We have always talked about getting a different place out of the city."

"That's true," Asher said. "I'm not sure how she will afford to feed that thing as it gets bigger on her salary."

Sage worried at the thought of taking care of the dragonling. But as she looked at the dragonling's adorable face and felt the warmth of its small body against her leg, she knew she couldn't abandon it.

"We'll figure it out," Sage said.

***

The din of the chatter and clinking of mugs inside the inn stopped when the door opened. All eyes focused on the group, and they could feel the tension in the air. Everyone stared at them, including the innkeeper, whose face was a mask of surprise. As the innkeeper moved toward them, the room turned their attention back to their tables, and the noise resumed.

"Prince Finn?" he whispered. "But, I thought... You..." He was unable to find the words to express his confusion.

Prince Finn smiled, a sad yet determined expression on his face. "We're back," he said, his voice gentle. "We just took the long way."

The innkeeper cleared his throat. "Well, this is certainly a surprise. What brings you back to my establishment? I thought you left."

"We are returning to Vishneel," Prince Finn said, his gaze flicking over to Prince Owen, who stood beside him, wearing the ropes they had used to bind Sage back in the forest. He looked as uncomfortable as everyone else did, and Sage felt a pang of sorrow for him.

"Ah," the innkeeper said. "I see." He paused, and scrutinized the group before meeting Prince Finn's gaze. "What do you intend to do with him?"

"That's up to him," Sage said. "But first, we will need our things you stored for us."

The innkeeper nodded. "Yes, it's all safe in the back room. I figured you'd be back for it sooner or later."

Prince Finn let out a relieved sigh. "Thank you." He turned to his companions, who all looked relieved too.

"Oh, and one more thing," the innkeeper said. He gestured awkwardly to the crowned prince, who was standing beside Sage. "I assume you brought him here as a prisoner. Am I correct?"

"Yes," Prince Finn said, "but he's under my protection for now. I won't let anyone hurt him and he will not be in anyone's way."

The innkeeper nodded again. "Very well. Then if you'll excuse me, I'll go fetch your things. Please, make yourselves at home."

Sage watched her companions, who all exchanged considering looks.

"Well," she said, "let's see if we can make the best of this situation. We have a lot to discuss."

No one spoke until Colby finally broke the silence.

"So," he said. "What are we going to do about Owen?"

Everyone's heads swiveled to the prince, who looked back at them expectantly.

"What do you mean?" Sage asked.

"I mean for the night. If he tries to escape while you're watching him, you might end up burning the entire place down," Colby teased Prince Finn.

"I'm not sure," he said.

There was a pause. "Why don't Colby, Asher and I have him stay in our room? We would be much more useful against him if he tried anything," Sawyer said.

"You would never do that, would you?" Asher teased with a poke at the crown prince's shoulder, which he quickly responded to with a growl.

The others all nodded, and Sage smiled. "Then that's what we'll do," Sawyer said. "Previous sleeping arrangements, then?"

Sage tried not to look too nervous as Prince Finn nodded to Sawyer's suggestion. She had romantic feelings for him now and was sure he had his own for her. She had figured she would have to sleep in the same room as him again, but this time it would be different.

She took a deep breath, working up the courage to accept, and then finally nodded, a small smile appearing.

"Alright," she said softly. Her friends all looked at her with smirks, teasing her but supporting their decision simultaneously.

The innkeeper returned with their stored items, and the group gathered their belongings and made their way up the stairs to their rooms. Asher, Sawyer, Colby, and Prince Owen entered the largest room, while Asher closed the door with a wink, leaving Sage and Prince Finn alone in the hallway. Prince Finn cleared his throat and opened the door to their room.

Once inside, he paused, silently gazing around the room.. "Are you sure you're alright with this?" he asked softly over his shoulder.

Sage nodded as her dragonling curled up under a small table with a vase of yellow flowers, her heart pounding as she took everything in. It was the same small room as before, cozy with a small bed pushed against the wall and a single window looking out into the night sky.

"Yes," she said finally, her voice barely above a whisper as she moved closer to him. "This will be okay."

Prince Finn smiled at her warmly before gesturing to the bed. "You're not going to try and sleep on the floor again, are you?"

Her heart beat faster as Prince Finn moved about the room, preparing for bed. He stripped off both his under and outer shirt and boots, revealing a sculpted chest that made her face flush even more.

She quickly unlaced her boots, crawled into bed, and buried herself in the cover, trying to compose herself. She heard him crawl into the other side and felt his warm presence beside her.

The room was quiet as they lay there, neither willing to break the silence between them.

Finally, Sage could take it no longer, and she cleared her throat softly. "Do you ... like me?" she asked tentatively.

Prince Finn gave a soft chuckle before turning onto his side to face her in the darkness. "I think it's obvious, honeybee," he murmured as he brushed a strand of hair away from Sage's face, their eyes meeting in the moonlight streaming through their window.

Sage's heart skipped a beat as their gazes locked, and she smiled shyly before looking away. Neither spoke for what seemed like an eternity, leaving only the sounds of their breathing.

"You're brave and strong," he said, breaking the silence with a compliment that made Sage blush even more than before. He felt for her hands before taking them as he gazed into her eyes with admiration shining in their depths. "You care about helping those in need and somehow decided that I was also worth helping. You have such an amazing soul, and the best thing that has come out of my curse."

Sage felt her face flush as she looked at Prince Finn. His words filled her with warmth, and she smiled shyly.

"You're an amazing leader," she said softly, "but you still know how to listen to others. You have such strength and courage, even when faced with insurmountable odds."

She paused, looking deep into his eyes. "When I first met you, you seemed so difficult, but now I've come to see that you're one of the kindest people I've ever met underneath it all."

Prince Finn brought it to his lips and gently kissed her knuckles.

"I'm glad fate let our paths cross," he murmured.

He pulled her to him until their faces were only inches apart, and their breath mingled in the darkness around them. She could feel the heat radiating off him and they both knew what was about to happen.

It was Prince Finn who finally leaned in and captured Sage's lips in a passionate kiss, sending sparks of excitement flying throughout her body.

Prince Finn kissed her deeply, his lips exploring hers with a hunger that matched hers. She wrapped her arms around his neck, pulling him closer as her fingers tangled in his hair.

"I want to be with you," Prince Finn murmured, his voice low and husky. Sage nodded, a fierce desire burning in her own eyes.

"Yes," she whispered, her voice barely audible. "I want that, too."

A Prince Before the King

S age and the others arrived at the palace gates late at night, their cloaks billowing in the cool breeze and hoods covering their tired faces. As soon as the guards spotted them, they leaped into action, drawing their swords and demanding the unknown travelers explain their presence.

"Quickly, now!" one of the guards said. "What is your business here?"

"We have apprehended the crowned prince," Prince Finn declared, his voice echoing with authority while his gaze swept over the guards. "He stands accused of a heinous crime and will face justice before the king and queen." His words reverberated through the night, their weight heavy with inevitability.

The guards exchanged a glance, their faces grim. "Very well, Your Highness. Follow us, then."

They escorted them into the palace and down a long, winding hallway to the throne room. Sage's heart pounded as they marched forward. She held the dragonling in her arms with her cloak wrapped tightly around them. They entered the throne room to find the king and queen seated upon their thrones, looking down upon them in displeasure.

"Explain yourselves," the king said, his voice ringing through the hall.

Prince Finn stepped forward. "Father, we have apprehended Prince Owen for his crimes. He attempted to poison the surviving dragons. We present him to you now for judgment."

The queen's eyes narrowed. "The dragons are extinct. How could he have poisoned something long dead since my father's time?"

"I've brought a witness," Prince Finn said as he gestured to Sage.

"Your-Your Highnesses," Sage began, her voice trembling, "it ... it is true. The crown prince came to me soon after his birthday ball; he forced me to make a poison for him."

She paused, her heart thundering. She could feel the weight of their stares and steeled herself. "He wanted me to make a poison capable of killing, but I changed the recipe at the last moment so that it would be harmless. I could not allow him to commit such an evil act. Especially without knowing who it was intended to be used on."

Prince Finn nodded. "I've been looking for the dragons for several years now. We followed the rumors of dragon sightings and eventually found them a few days ago. Unfortunately, we arrived too late to stop the crown prince from attempting his plan."

The king and queen exchanged a look before turning their attention back to Sage and Finn. "If what you say is true," the king said after clearing his throat, "then this is a grave matter indeed. Do you have proof of the dragons or poison?"

Sage slowly opened her cloak to reveal the dragonling, its bright amber eyes shining with a look of trust. It chirped at the king and queen before nuzzling its head into Sage's stomach.

"Your Highnesses," she began, "I have bonded with this dragonling after saving it from the crowned prince's attack."

The king and queen looked on in shock as Sage continued to explain what had happened. "None of the dragons were actually harmed. I changed the poison recipe to ensure that."

"Why did you do this?" the king asked, his voice low and dangerous.

"How dare you!" Prince Owen roared, his face burning. "I did it to protect this kingdom; the dragons had slaughtered fae before! They would have done the same again if I hadn't taken action! It was my duty as the future monarch!" He turned his raging eyes upon Sage. "And you! You gave me false poison, lying about its effects!"

Sage shied away from his fury but stood her ground. "Your Highness," she calmly said, "I could not allow such an evil act."

Prince Owen's blistering rage grew, and Sage could feel the dragonling growing more agitated. It puffed a little plume of smoke from its nostrils at the crowned prince before Sage hushed it.

The crowned prince scowled at Sage, his face red with rage.

"This has gone far enough!" Prince Finn interjected, stepping between them. You will not address her like that again."

Prince Owen's eyes widened in shock before he gritted his teeth and stepped back. He cast a sinister look toward me.

"Do you really think that you, a spare heir, can tell me, the crown prince, what to do?"

The king's and queen's expressions showed alarm as the two men squared off against each other. The power radiating from them was palpable, and it seemed the fight might erupt into violence at any moment.

Suddenly, a magical barrier appeared around the two princes and Sage, separating them from the rest of the room. Sage stepped back in shock as flames erupted from the crown prince's hands and began to lick around their feet. The dragonling chirped, pressing itself against Sage for protection.

A familiar presence entered her mind telling her not to worry; she wouldn't get burned because of their bond.

The brothers clashed, the air around them crackling with the intensity of their battle.

Flames erupted from Prince Finn's fingers, engulfing both princes in a billowing wall of smoke.

Sage breathed in the acrid scent of charred wood as she watched the brothers battle with wild abandon. The dragonling clung to her, its tiny wings flapping frantically against her.

Prince Finn's fingertips began to shimmer and glow as if summoning flames from within. Gray smoke billowed from his hands, and the smell of more burning wood filled the air.

His grasp on the power seemed to strengthen and grow until sparks began to fly around him as if he had become a bonfire. In an instant, he was engulfed by a sphere of searing flames that burned hotter than any fire she had ever witnessed.

The heat forced his brother back, howling in pain, and leaving Finn standing alone encased in a fireball.

Sage could only watch in horror as Prince Finn's hands turned gray and the fire spread up his arms like wildfire. She screamed as he fell to the ground, his flames extinguishing. She rushed to his side, kneeling, while tears streamed from her eyes.

The dragonling jumped from Sage's arms and nuzzled against Prince Finn's face. It chirped in distress, and moved to his chest. Sage held her breath, wondering if he were still alive.

She reached into her pocket and retrieved one of the bottles Rachel had left for Prince Finn's treatment at the inn. She cradled his head in one hand and helped him drink the more potent dose.

Her tears continued as she prayed this would be enough to reverse the damage.

With a gasp, Prince Finn opened his eyes, alive but weakened from the ordeal. Sage let out a relieved sigh before turning to Prince Owen, who was trying to regain his composure after being bested by his brother's magic.

The king and queen came down the steps leading to their thrones, their faces drawn with worry as they surveyed their sons' conditions. "What did you just give him?" the king asked. Prince Finn's eyes were gray and wide instead of their usual brown.

Sage offered the bottle to him, which he took and sniffed.

"I've been working on it to avoid Prince Finn becoming a full gargoyle. The last two treatments have made improvements," Sage said, pausing to sniffle back tears, "and we hope he will be cured soon."

The queen's eyes widened, her gaze flickering between Sage and Prince Finn. "This is quite remarkable," she said in a hushed tone. "I had no idea such a cure was even possible."

Sage bowed her head, her cheeks burning at the unexpected praise. She had never been one for attention, but it was hard to ignore the weight of the queen's words.

"My dear, you must be exhausted," she said, her face softening. "We'll have someone take you home so you can rest."

"Allow us," Asher said, moving closer and slightly bowing.

"Is Prince Finn coming with us?" Sawyer asked.

The king looked over Prince Finn, taking in the slowly receding gray on his arms. "If you allow us to send you back in a carriage with a palace physician, I will allow it. It appears you have the only treatment that can help him now."

The king nodded, and Asher and Colby quickly moved to pick up the now unconscious Prince Finn.

"Let's get him back home," Asher said, while they adjusted their grip on the prince's body.

Sage heard the king give orders to have Prince Owen thrown into a cell below to await a full trial as she headed to the throne room's exit.

The group made their way through the castle and into a large carriage. A royal physician waited for them inside. Though weak and pale, Prince Finn's breathing was steady as he slept. Sage sank into a nearby seat, allowing exhaustion to overtake her.

Her eyes grew heavy as she dozed off, though her mind remained active with worry over the man who had won her heart.

***

Sage smiled when she saw Piper and Will standing in the park from across the path. She had not seen them in so long and was happy to be reunited. She was about to call out to them when she noticed the dragonling wrap itself around her leg.

The dragonling was still small and silver but growing quickly. Sage had enjoyed caring for it since the day it had hatched, and it had become her constant companion and friend.

"Oh my gosh!" Piper said. "Is this your dragonling?"

Sage nodded and smiled proudly. "This is them."

"It's so cute," Will said, trying to reach out and pet it, but the dragonling hissed at him, and he quickly drew back his hand.

Sage laughed. "It's still a bit skittish around people it doesn't know."

"It's understandable," Piper said. "It's still so young."

Will laid a bright blue blanket on the park's green grass, and Piper placed a large basket in the center. They all sat and began pulling the food and drinks from it, carefully keeping it away from the dragonling.

"So," Piper said finally, "we've wanted to ask you... Are you coming back to work at the library anytime soon?"

Sage shook her head. "No," she said softly. "It's not something I can do right now." She tossed a stick for the dragonling to catch, careful not to throw it too close to any others in the park. "We are bonded, and as far as I can tell, it can't leave my side. I'm unsure what element the dragonling is; I'm guessing fire, and a library is no place for that."

Piper pulled Sage's favorite blue and white cup from the basket along with a sealed bottle. "I was afraid of that. Keep this, I paid for it, so it wasn't stolen or anything."

The smell of white chocolate and lavender filled Sage's nose as Piper opened the bottle and poured it into her cup.

"Piper, you are the best friend a girl could have. Thank you."

The dragonling returned, a stick between its long sharp teeth with its tail wagging behind it like a scaled puppy. It promptly dropped its prize beside Sage and sniffed at the cup of coffee, flicking its tongue to sneak a taste.

"Excuse you?!" Sage laughed. "You are much too young to have coffee already." She tossed the stick again and turned her attention back to her friends as the dragonling happily chased it once again.

Will and Piper exchanged glances, and Sage knew what they were thinking.

"So..." Piper said slowly. "Is it... Are you ... happy?"

Sage looked away, a blush rising to her cheeks. "Yes," she said, meeting her friends' gaze. "I am happy."

Piper and Will smiled at her, clearly relieved.

"That's great," Piper said. "We're so happy for you."

Will nodded. "Yeah. We just want you to be happy."

Sage smiled, feeling a warmth spread through her.

"So," Will said, looking at the dragonling, "does it have a name?"

Sage shook her head. "Not yet. I'm still waiting for it to tell me its name. I don't even know what gender it is. I haven't had a chance to find a book that could tell me how to identify that."

Will grinned. "Well, I've got a suggestion. How about ... Merp?"

The dragonling returned with the stick and let out a little huff. Sage laughed.

"I don't think it likes that one," she said.

"Maybe we should let the dragonling choose its name," Piper suggested.

Sage nodded. "Yes, that's what I was planning on doing. Once it's ready, I'm sure it'll tell me."

Paige and Will smiled, though Sage could see Piper held a look of concern.

"So..." Piper said carefully. "You leave tomorrow?"

Sage nodded. "Yes, the dragonling will soon be too big to be in the city, so we'll have to move. But we'll keep the house here so we can visit."

Will smiled. "That sounds great. We'll miss you, but seeing you visit will be good."

As they talked, the dragonling snuggled up against Sage's leg as if sensing she was sad. She ran her fingers over its soft, warm scales taking comfort from their bond.

"I'll be back soon," Sage said, trying to keep her voice steady. "I promise."

"We know," Piper said, leaning forward and hugging her. "Just be careful out there."

Will hugged her next. "And make sure to come back in one piece," he grinned.

Piper pulled her back into a tight embrace. "We'll miss you," she said softly.

The group hugged, trying not to disturb the dragonling, and Sage held back tears pricking her eyes. "I'll miss you too," she whispered.

Happily Ever After

S age looked at her friends, filled with a thrilling mix of anticipation and competition. They were gathered around a table in their new home outside Nectars Embrace's land, the game of Everhunt laid out before them. Prince Finn sat next to her, his gaze focused on the game in front of them.

It had become a weekly habit since the Charming Four moved to the country to invite Rachel and Michael over for a night of food and games. They had become friends with Freddy and would often show up together. After his treatments started to reverse his damage, he had more hours in the day when he wasn't a gargoyle. Along with Asher, Sawyer, and Colby, Freddy had moved into a small tenant home on the land the guild had purchased, insisting that Sage and Prince Finn should have their own space. Sage couldn't help but appreciate the thoughtfulness.

Prince Finn gave her a sly smile and winked, causing her heart to flutter. She blushed and returned to the game, determined to concentrate on the task. As her gaze settled on the cards, she felt the presence of her dragonling at her feet, snuggled up against her leg.

"Let's make this interesting then," Prince Finn said, breaking the silence while a thrill ran through Sage as his gaze lingered on her. "If I win, we will be married in the country before my family can approve. A small wedding with only friends and immediate family. If you win, we will have a grand royal wedding as you wanted and make my parents foot the bill."

There was a collective gasp around the table, and Sage's cheeks flushed. She glanced at the others, who were all watching her. She hesitated, unsure of how to respond.

"Are you asking me to marry you?" Sage asked.

Prince Finn pulled a small gold band from his pocket and held it before her. "If you will have me," he said with a smile.

"All right, then," she said, her voice steady. "Let's do this."

The game commenced, and for a time, everything seemed to fade away as Sage became absorbed in the game. She chose a fire dragon and began selecting her hoard items and spells.

"What are you naming your player?" Rachel's voice drew Sage back to the other players at the table.

"Excuse me?" Sage asked.

"The dragon you are playing," Rachel said, pointing to the card in front of Sage. "What will you name it? It makes the game much more interesting if you play with named dragons. Don't you think?"

"I don't know. I hadn't thought about it."

"I'm voting for Fluffy," Sawyer teased.

"No! Smokey," Colby added.

"I've got it," Freddy joined in, "barebone. Because he will eat you down to the bone."

"You're all terrible. You know that?" Sage said, trying not to laugh. "Now you all have to keep your own kindly offered dragon names for your own dragons. I'm thinking ... Starblaze."

The familiar sensation of her dragonling communicating with her filled her mind. A sense of approval. Sage scooted her chair to look at the little dragonling at her feet.

"You like that? Do you want to be Starblaze?"

The dragonling lifted its head momentarily, let out a little happy chirp, and tucked its nose under its tail.

"I guess we take that as a yes," Prince Finn offered.

Sage laughed. "I guess so!"

The game was intense and fast-paced, and Sage worried over her moves. As the game progressed, she found her fortunes shifting. She began to amass a hoard of gold pieces while Prince Finn's fortunes seemed to dwindle until they both had an impressive collection of coins, and the game entered its final phase.

Prince Finn made a bold move, attempting to take Sage's hoard. But Sage was prepared. She had been holding onto a powerful spell card, waiting for the perfect moment to use it. With a sly grin, she placed the card down and Prince Finn's dragon burned to a crisp, leaving him with nothing but a pile of ash where his hoard once stood.

The room erupted in cheers and laughter as everyone celebrated Sage's victory. She smiled proudly and high-fived each of her friends, feeling a wave of satisfaction.

Prince Finn leaned in close, his face glowing. "Congratulations, honeybee."

Sage's heart skipped a beat as their eyes met. He leaned even closer, and she could feel his warm breath on her skin. "You should get the biggest wedding dress you can find," he whispered as he slid the ring onto her hand.

Sage blushed and couldn't help the smile that spread across her face. She leaned in and planted a soft kiss on his lips. The moment felt surreal, as if time had stopped just for them.

When they finally pulled apart, they looked around at their friends, who were staring at them with amusement. Sage laughed nervously before turning back to Prince Finn with a bright smile; she knew she'd never face it alone, no matter what happened next.

WHITE CHOCOLATE
LAVENDER LATTE

1-2 Tablespoons Honey
1-2 Tablespoons Lavender Simple
Syrup
1-2 Tablespoons White Chocolate
Syrup
1 Cup Strong Brewed Coffee
1/4-1/2 cup heavy whipping cream

Brew your coffee first.
In a mug or cup pour about ¼ to ½ cup cup of heavy cream, 1 tablespoon white chocolate syrup, 1 tablespoon of honey, and 1 tablespoon lavender simple syrup. If you want stronger lavender flavor you adjust the combination to 1 tablespoon of honey and 2 tablespoons of lavender simple syrup.
Froth the cream. Pour in the coffee.
(Torini makes a gread white chocolate drizzle/syrup you can use)

LAVENDER SIMPLE SYRUP

1 Cup Water

1 Cup White Sugar

2 Tablespoons Lavender Petals

Measure your ingredients into a pot over low heat on the stove. Stir occassionally until all of the sugar disolves. Turn off heat and cover allowing the lavender to steep for 5-10 minutes. Strain out the lavender petals and put into a container to store.

Bee Classifications

Draqium Bee – an angry type that easily swarms if left unattended for a season. Best partnered with a fire mage and attributed plants.

Will rob nearby hives if they are found to be weak, or small of their honey. Will eat excess honey if it's not removed immediately

Vidali Honey Bee – Very freindly. Needs very little smoke or clothing for protection. Large hives. Preferrs warm weather. Keep in double walled hive to protect from elements. Best matched with earth mage.
Does not like overly sweet nectar. Best combined with herbs and vegetables. Swarms early

Tagium Bee – Most adapted to cold weatehr. Partner with Ice mages. Easily breeds with other bees to make hybrids. Careful because it can honey with unintended and different medicinal purposes. This breed always has a queen and a princess. Must use both to move a hive.
Very large breed of bee. Extra fuzzy with small wings. Short distance for flight. Easily catch diseases so keep away from other bees.

Grison Bee – Small bee that can not become a hybrid. Best for non magical treatments.
Creates best wax for cadles, soaps and water proofing. Long tongue, can use plants no other bee can use. Creates honey that combines magical elements from other breeds

Bee Habits and Helps

Match the smoke to the intended medicinal outcome of the hive. Type of wood chips, pine needles...

Comb Uses
- Skin Smoothing
- Digested for antifungel
- Treat Sunburn and Rashes
- Use as beauty (tint lips and cheeks)

Double Walled Hive

Watch for Skunks! They eat bees

Use hive tool to open hive. Bees glue everything together with propolis

Only feed bees honey from own hive, or disease can spread

Feed Bees honey and sugar during cold to make sure they get enough nutrients until they can naturally get their own.

Is there one better than the others for different hives?

Plants vs Magic Type

Fire Related Plants
- White Wintercress Rose
- Silent Holly
- Mimic Ink Plant
- Shadow Lily
- Obisphire (yellow only)
- Dire Sorrel
- Macquetra's Ophillium

Marsh Olive and Whisper Rose can be used for any magical affinity for most treatments

Earth Magic Related Plants
- Creeping Windroot
- Carrots
- Ginger
- Tundra Poppy
- Mocking Roadweed

Never Use These on Mages!
- Swallow Wart
- Hovering Collard
- Grave Itchweed
- Faregon

- Test be used with Ash Water, R Dirt Helps amplify the reversal

Passhy Chilling Rankweed Treatment of Ice mage for Gorgoile?

Water and Ice Magic Related Plants
- Grey Lavender
- Imperial Stickwood
- Sacred Dewberry
- Thranium
- Stinking Rose Vine
- Green Laurel

Behind the Scenes

I thought it would be fun to share a few be-
hind-the-scenes about the inspiration for this
book. First, let's talk about Twinkle Twinkle Little
Dragon. As I began this book I knew the vibes I wanted to try and go with but was still piecing the world
together. One night my then 3-year-old daughter
thought it would be so funny to trick mommy during singing time for bed. She batted up at me with
her long lashes and had a mischievous grin when
she asked me if I could sing Twinkle Twinkle Little
Dragon. Her face morphed into excitement when I
started singing a song combining Twinkle Twinkle
Little Star with Old MacDonald where it changed
the animal for every verse and she would get to pick
which one that was.

After tucking her into bed and heading downstairs
to write, because let's be honest, half the time I
function on a vampire's schedule, my overly tired
brain thought "wouldn't it be funny if the gargoyle
made them sing that to check out books?" At the
time I didn't know Freddy could shift or even what
the curse was that she needed to overcome.

I do admit that was currently on my third rewatch of Meteor Garden when the idea of this book came to me. I knew I needed something light, fun, and sassy to write to balance out a darker project I was working on and stumbled on a post on Facebook by a reader in a reader group asking for book recs that had the almost why choose trope. They listed a bunch of shows including Meteor Garden and no one had any book recs for it. Even I couldn't think of one. My mind started down my list of "Wouldn't it be funny if..." and the idea formed for a mage guild of 4 guys needing help from 1 girl in a cozy high fantasy setting.

Even 1/4 of the way through the book I still didn't know how to fix the curse. Was it really magic? Was it something tangible? What did they need to do to fix it? Thank you tik tok, I stumbled on a post about weird things about honey. After digging into Google down a wild brain squirrel chase I stumbled on the mellified man. It's definitely not cozy so I knew I couldn't write it in the book (seriously, google it with the warning that it's super gross) but that got me thinking about the medicinal uses of honey, how honey is made by bees and wondering what other types of unique and powerful honey there were.

That's when I stumbled on mad honey. Did you know it's a real thing? None of the elements of it are exaggerated. It's bright red and can kill someone if they eat too much of it.

Thank You!

First, thank you to my readers. This has been such an incredible journey for me and I know I would not have made it this far if it wasn't for you. Your emails, reviews, social media posts and honestly just reads are what keep me going when my characters decide to fight me.

Cassie, you are the best kid a mom could ask for. I love how creative your young mind is. Twinkle Twinkle little dragon would never have happened if it wasn't for you trying to trick me by asking me to sing it before bed. Making up a song on the spot is never easy, but this has to be a favorite of mine.

Andrew, the fact that you believe in me as much as you do means the world to me. You are my other half, my love and one of the best decisions I've ever made.

Jenny, you saved me yet again. You are the best!

Julie, you know just how much I appreciate you. Last minute things being sent your way and you were done faster than I was ready. Thank you!

To the other authors releasing with me in the Starry Kingdoms of the Fae series, thank you for putting up with my wild ideas and being willing to go along for the ride. This has become so much more than I imagined it could and I can't wait to see how our future releases go!

To the rest of my family and my inlaws, thank you. Your support is greatly appreciated. As is your willingness to sometimes allow me to talk out the imaginary worlds I'm creating as I create them.

About Author

A woman who grew up in the mountains of Oregon and Idaho and settled down with her introverted prince charming and their book loving toddler in North Carolina. Although JD Magnetra is not her first alter ego (James Blonde, Sky, and Magnetra are all names given to me by now loved family, coworkers and social media) it is one that she enjoys exploring. But that's not what this books about. This book is from the real world of Jamie Dalton.

She's had a lifelong love affair with mint chocolate truffle cake, crispy chicken bites, all forms of pasta, deviled eggs... and now I'm hungry. Perhaps this is a little part of why all of her books have at least one recipe from within the story included in the back pages. She grew up dreaming of that perfect chocolate cake that Matilda helped eat. Of the feasts from the Lord of the Rings and the picnics in every single Jane Austen book. So she figured why not include a little sneak peek into how she viewed the worlds she created so readers could see, feel and taste it too! Promise, there will never be any olives. Olives are disgusting.

Ever since the first time she could read The Berenstian Bears and the Messy Room, she has loved books. Fantasy, romance, science fiction, biographies, historical... in all honestly most books she enjoys. Well, other than thriller and horror which is sort of funny considering that her first book published was listed by Amazon as fantasy horror. A category she quickly remedied considering she is easily scared and can't even handle watching Alice in Wonderland or the end of The Little Mermaid.

Welcome to the inner workings of this authors mind as she entertains herself with fantastical stories in the hopes that someone else may be entertained as well.